ZAC POWER

ZAC'S BIGGEST EVER HITS! VOLUME 3

BY H.I. LARRY

Hardie Grant
EGMONT

Zac's Biggest Ever Hits! Volume 3
published in 2019 by
Hardie Grant Egmont
Ground Floor, Building 1, 658 Church Street
Richmond, Victoria 3121, Australia
www.hardiegrantegmont.com

A catalogue record for this
book is available from the
National Library of Australia

Text copyright © 2019 H.I. Larry
Illustration and design copyright © 2019 Hardie Grant Egmont

Front cover illustration by Jon Davis
Cover design by Pooja Desai
Internal illustrations by Craig Phillips and Marcelo Baez
Internal illustrations inked by Latifah Cornelius

Printed in Australia by McPherson's Printing Group,
Maryborough, Victoria

1 3 5 7 9 10 8 6 4 2

The paper in this book is FSC® certified.
FSC® promotes environmentally responsible,
socially beneficial and economically viable
management of the world's forests.

CONTENTS

ZAC POWER

FOSSIL FURY

CHAPTER 1

'Zac, could you please carry this bag of manure?'

Zac Power and his mum were at the garden centre. It wasn't the sort of place you'd expect to find a top-secret spy. But that's exactly what Zac was.

Zac's whole family worked for an elite spy agency called the Government

Investigation Bureau, or GIB for short.

Being a spy was supposed to be cool. The last time Zac checked, carrying a bag of manure was not cool – especially when you were wearing your brand new Axe Grinder T-shirt!

'Yuck!' said Zac. 'Do I have to?'

'Yes,' said his mum. You could tell from the look on her face why her secret spy name was Agent Bum Smack. 'I'm carrying all these pot plants. Actually, that reminds me – it's your turn to take out the compost when we get home.'

Zac groaned. The compost smelled even worse than manure! He picked up the heavy plastic bag of Grundy's Garden

Grower and followed his mum out to the car park.

Zac's nose twitched as he walked outside. He could smell something. Not the manure … something good. There was a sausage sizzle in the car park!

Sweet, thought Zac. *I've earned a snack.*

'I'm just going to get a sausage,' he told his mum, once he'd dumped the manure in the car boot.

As Zac walked over to the sausage sizzle, he noticed something strange. The guy flipping the sausages was staring right at him.

Zac's spy senses tingled. He didn't recognise the man at all, but the man sure seemed to recognise him.

'Hello,' said the man, handing Zac a sausage in bread. 'Why don't you help yourself to some extra-spicy chilli mustard sauce? It's your favourite, isn't it?'

Zac raised an eyebrow and nodded. How did the man know?

Zac reached for the plastic bottle on the table and held it over the sausage in bread. But when he squeezed the bottle, nothing came out.

'Hey, it's empty!' Zac said.

'Try again,' said the man, winking at him.

Zac frowned and gave the bottle a shake. Something rattled inside it.

He glanced around to make sure no-one was looking, and then twisted the lid off. He tipped the contents into his hand.

All that came out was a silver object shaped like a coin. A GIB mission disk!

'Hello, Agent Rock Star,' whispered the man behind the barbecue, giving Zac a small nod. 'I'm Agent Hot Dog.'

At that moment, Zac saw a Mike's Mobile Mowing van come swerving through the car park. It was one of those vans that came to your house to do your gardening – except this one had tinted windows.

Obviously, this was no ordinary gardening van.

It pulled up right behind Zac, and the doors flew open. Then he heard a familiar voice from inside.

'Get in, Zac!' said his brother Leon.

This could only mean one thing, thought Zac. *A new mission!*

CHAPTER 2

Zac climbed into the back of the van. Just as he'd thought, there wasn't a lawn mower or whipper snipper in sight. Instead, the walls were covered with wires, computer monitors and blinking lights.

Zac knew he was inside a GIB Mobile Technology Lab. His brother Leon, also known as Agent Tech Head, was standing at a small workbench. Leon was a computer whiz, science whiz and history whiz, all rolled up into one nerdy package. He didn't really go on missions. Instead he stayed behind, getting information to Zac, working on new gadgets, and somehow being uncool and useful at the same time.

The MTL doors swung shut, and the van started moving again. For a second Zac wondered who was driving. Then he remembered that Leon usually set the MTL to autopilot. That kept Leon's hands free for doing what he loved most – tinkering with gadgets.

Leon made a final adjustment to the new piece of GIB hardware he was working on, then looked up at Zac. 'Have you read your new mission yet?'

'I'm just about to,' said Zac, finishing off his sausage in bread. He wiped his hands on his pants and pulled out his SpyPad.

GIB agents never went anywhere without their SpyPad. It was the most useful spy gadget in the world – a super-charged tablet with a video phone, chemical analyser, laser, GPS and loads of other features.

Zac sat up on Leon's workbench, because he knew that annoyed him. He messaged his mum to let her know where he'd gone, and then slid the mission disk into his SpyPad.

CLASSIFIED

MISSION INITIATED: 2 P.M.

CURRENT TIME: 2.33 P.M.

The evil scientist Dr Drastic claims to have hatched a live dinosaur at the Bladesville BioDome. He will present the dinosaur to the International Science Council tomorrow afternoon.

However, GIB suspects that Drastic will attack the Council instead. He has planned something called Operation Extinct for 2 p.m. tomorrow.

YOUR MISSION:
Confirm that the dinosaur is a fake. Find out what Operation Extinct is and stop it.

~ END ~

Zac looked up at Leon, his mouth hanging open. 'Dr Drastic is saying he's brought a dinosaur back to life? That's impossible!'

Zac knew that Dr Drastic was a brilliant scientist, but hatching a live dinosaur was a stretch even for him.

Leon shrugged. 'It's not entirely impossible,' he said. 'They died out millions of years ago, but some of them left behind fossils. If Dr Drastic found a really well-preserved fossil with bits of DNA, he maybe could have used the genetic sequence to …'

Zac could tell from the gleam in Leon's eye that he was going to explain exactly how Drastic might have done it. In precise detail. Possibly with diagrams.

'OK, OK,' Zac said quickly. He had to stop Leon now. 'I don't need to know the details. Just tell me whether you think it's a real dinosaur or not.'

Leon thought for a moment. 'Probably not, but you need to find out for sure. If it's a fake, then Drastic is obviously up to something. And we know he's wanted to take down the council for ages.'

Zac nodded. 'What kind of dinosaur is it supposed to be?'

'A Spinosaurus,' said Leon. 'A meat-eater, very dangerous – and even bigger than a T-Rex.'

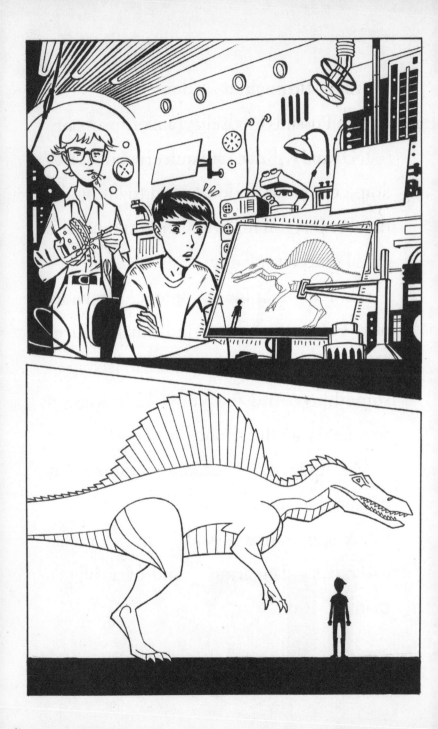

'Bigger?' Zac asked.

Leon nodded. 'Longer, taller, probably faster – and with a head like a crocodile. But don't worry, it's only a baby-sized one.'

Leon shivered excitedly, and then glanced at the speedometer on the dashboard. 'I think we're going to need a bit more speed to get to Bladesville on time,' he added. 'Do you feel like driving?'

Zac grinned. 'Always,' he said, sitting down at the controls.

Whether the dinosaur was real or not, there was no time to waste when Dr Drastic was involved!

CHAPTER

Zac nudged the controls forward and gave the van an extra burst of speed. He'd been driving for a couple of hours, and the GPS screen on the dashboard showed that Bladesville was just up ahead.

A couple of raindrops splashed on the windscreen as dark clouds gathered in the sky. It looked like a storm was coming.

'OK,' said Leon, pointing to a section of the GPS screen. 'Drastic has been working out of the BioDome on the other side of the city, so we need to head there.'

Zac knew the BioDome was a special greenhouse where nerds like Leon studied different environments. It was weird to think of a garden growing in the middle of Bladesville's skyscrapers and dirty alleys.

Zac weaved the van through the noisy traffic on the outskirts of Bladesville. Even at the edge of the city, there were traffic jams everywhere.

He heard Leon's SpyPad beeping. He glanced back to see Leon frowning at his screen.

'GIB needs me back at HQ,' Leon said, looking up. 'And we'll never get anywhere in this traffic. You'd better stop the van and go the rest of the way on your own.'

Zac groaned. 'But the BioDome's on the other side of the city!'

Still, he pulled the van over to the side of the road and got up from the controls.

'I know,' said Leon, holding up a pair of thin, grey, metallic-looking straps. 'So it's a good thing I made you these!'

Leon wrapped the straps around Zac's hands. Each strap was wirelessly connected to a small suction pad.

'They're called SwingBands,' said Leon, sticking the suction pad to the back of

Zac's neck. 'Each band contains a tiny photonic cell and a super-strong magnet. The cell fires a focused beam that can magnetise a surface up to 200 metres away, and then –'

'Got it,' said Zac, rolling his eyes. 'It's like an invisible grappling hook that I can control with my hands.'

'Exactly!' said Leon. 'If you get your timing right, you can swing yourself through city streets, jungles, desert canyons – anywhere you can find a wall.'

'How do I activate them?' asked Zac.

'Follow me,' said Leon, pushing open the back door of the van. 'Now, hold out your hands carefully. And whatever you do, don't blink until I tell you.'

Zac sighed. He hated being told what to do by his nerdy older brother. But he was itching to see how these things worked.

Leon tapped the power stud on the back of each SwingBand. Then he stretched Zac's arm out as far as it could go.

'It's all controlled with your arm movements and brainwaves,' said Leon. 'The brain is just a big computer, after all. Point your palm where you want to go, hold your arm straight, then blink. It won't take you long to get into the, er, *swing* of it. OK?'

Zac ignored Leon's joke. He aimed his palm at the side of a building, stared at a window five floors up … and then blinked.

WHOOSH!

Suddenly Zac was whisked from the back of the van and flew through the air – straight towards the side of the building!

'Swing yourself to the next one, before you go splat!' he heard Leon yell from the ground.

Zac threw his arm toward a building on the other side of the road – ten floors up this time.

He fixed his eyes on where he wanted to go, blinked, and –

WHOOSH!

He changed direction just before he smashed into the side of the building.

Aim, blink …

WHOOSH! WHOOSH!

Zac was swinging between buildings, fifteen floors up now. Cars and trucks inched along the road below, totally unaware of the secret agent zipping through the air above them like Spiderman.

Then Zac remembered something.

How in the world do I STOP these things?

Zac's SpyPad was beeping. It was probably Leon calling. Zac couldn't reach the SpyPad, so he activated the hands-free control.

'Authorise SpyPad: Agent Rock Star,' he shouted. 'Open message!'

'Zac, it's Leon!' came a voice from the SpyPad. 'I forgot to tell you two things! One, press the stud on the back of the SwingBands to power them down. Two, don't use them the whole way to the BioDome – you should save some power for later!'

Zac groaned. 'Now he tells me!'

CHAPTER

Zac was hurtling straight towards an apartment block. *I guess I should switch off the SwingBands soon,* he thought. *But how do I make a safe landing?*

Then Zac noticed a set of metal fire escape steps on the side of the apartments. On instinct, Zac flicked off his SwingBands and threw himself at the railing – a split second before he slammed into the wall!

I am awesome, thought Zac. Then he realised he was still dangling on the edge of the fire escape – 15 floors up!

Zac used all his strength to pull himself over the railing and onto the steps.

Now that he'd stopped flying through the air, Zac got his breath back and checked the time on his SpyPad. It was 7 p.m.

Better get a move on, thought Zac. He climbed down the fire escape steps and jumped to the ground. He found himself in a dark alley, next to an overflowing rubbish bin. Zac wrinkled his nose. *Why has today been so smelly?*

He turned to head out of the laneway.

Then he heard a rumble of thunder. Moments later, heavy rain began falling from the sky. Lightning flickered around the tops of skyscrapers, and Zac could feel the crackle of electricity in the air.

Oh great, he thought. *An electrical storm. I'll have to wait this one out.*

Zac ducked under a ledge, hoping to stay there until the rain eased up. But instead, the downpour got so bad that Zac could barely see.

Great, he thought, shivering. *Standing around under a fire escape, with nothing but a smelly bin for company!*

Then Zac remembered he was carrying a SafeCrate, one of GIB's latest inventions.

He reached into his pocket and pulled out a small grey object with dimples all over it like a golf ball.

Zac ducked back into the alley. He squeezed the SafeCrate three times and put it on the ground behind the dumpster, resting it flat on one of the dimples.

The ball got bigger and bigger until it came up to Zac's hip. Zac reached out and pressed three of the dimples in a special order know only to GIB agents.

A hatch opened in the side of the sphere. Zac crawled inside and shut the door. The inside of the ball was small, but the walls were fitted with inflatable padding for comfort.

At least Zac would stay warm and dry for a while. The only problem was that he'd be bored out of his brain!

Zac got out his SpyPad. A good spy always used his time wisely. Even though what Zac really wanted to do was load up a game of *Crazy Cannibal Cavemen*, he decided to do some dinosaur research instead. There was still a chance that Drastic's dinosaur was real, after all.

Zac set the SpyPad to Research Mode and typed in 'Spinosaurus'.

An article came up from GIBpedia, the GIB information database. Zac scrolled through pages and pages of text, looking for useful information. He couldn't help noticing that most of the info had been added by a certain Agent Tech Head.

My brother is such a nerd, thought Zac, yawning.

According to the main page, the Spinosaurus had died out about 100 million years ago. One hundred million years!

Zac wondered sleepily what it would be like to see a real live Spinosaurus. He still couldn't believe Dr Drastic had managed to create a whole dinosaur – even a baby one – just from some old fossil.

Zac scrolled through a few more pages. He yawned again. He'd already done a lot of research.

I should probably shut my eyes for a moment,

he told himself as the rain pelted down on the SafeCrate. *I need to be alert in case Drastic's dinosaur is real. I don't want to end up being its lunch!*

When Zac opened his eyes a few hours later, the first thing he noticed was the silence. The rain had stopped pounding down.

Zac tried to stretch a bit, but it was pretty cramped inside the SafeCrate. Then he glanced at the SpyPad.

It was 9 a.m. the next day. He'd slept for way too long, and now there were only five hours left to complete his mission!

Oh no, he thought with a groan. *Leon's going to kill me!*

Zac slipped out of the SafeCrate and pressed another combination of buttons to shrink it down to size.

Then he put it back in his pocket and started racing on foot through the busy streets of Bladesville.

It took Zac more than an hour to reach Dr Drastic's BioDome on the other side of the city.

He slowed down to a jog when he saw it up ahead, surrounded by white and silver skyscrapers.

It was a massive glass dome with a sliding metallic door on one side. Through the glass, Zac could see a lush, colourful jungle.

Tourists were making their way inside. Zac joined the end of the line, using his spy skills to blend in with one of the families. For all Zac knew, Dr Drastic could be watching his every move. The line took forever to get to the ticket counter.

As Zac shuffled closer, he saw a sign near the entrance:

BLADESVILLE BIODOME
OPEN TO THE PUBLIC
9 a.m. – 1 p.m.
CHILDREN ADMITTED FREE

It's weird that Drastic doesn't keep the BioDome open all day, Zac thought. *He'd make more money from the Spinosaurus if he did.*

Zac finally made it into the BioDome and slipped off into the crowd.

He'd been in real jungles before, and if he didn't know better he'd think he was in one now. The air was hot, and the dome was filled with snaking vines, strange-looking flowers and thick trees.

There was an excited crowd gathering around a small wire fence nearby.

Zac was just wondering what they were looking at when he heard a squawking, croaking noise.

He peered through the crowd, trying

to work out where the bizarre sound was coming from.

And then he saw it.

Dr Drastic's baby dinosaur!

CHAPTER 5

Zac's mouth dropped open.

The spinosaurus was taller than Zac. *That's hardly baby-sized,* he thought. Its head was shaped like a crocodile's, just like Leon had said, and it had a long mouth full of sharp teeth.

The creature stood on a pair of thick legs, with a powerful-looking tail behind.

Sticking out the front of its body were two stubby arms, each ending in a set of long, curved claws. Along its spine was a sharp fin.

Zac was impressed. It certainly looked like a real dinosaur, not that he'd ever seen one before. Still, he had a nagging feeling that something wasn't right. But what?

One of the staff from the BioDome was standing by, keeping a close eye on the creature and making sure no-one tried to get over the fence. Every now and then the spinosaurus let out another weird squawk, making everyone gasp.

Zac edged closer to the fence for a better look. A TV crew was putting cameras and spotlights and sound equipment into position around the dinosaur.

Zac recognised the logo on the side of the cameras. This crew was from *Creepy Creatures*, Leon's favourite TV show! Zac knew his brother would be super jealous.

He turned his attention back to the baby spinosaurus. He watched closely as it bared its teeth and squawked again. It seemed to shudder ever so slightly when it moved its head.

It was as though the spinosaurus was somehow almost … mechanical.

Suddenly, someone shoved a microphone in Zac's face. All the *Creepy Creatures* cameras swung in his direction.

'So, little boy,' said the man holding the microphone, 'are you a big fan of dinosaurs? Have you come to see the baby spinosaurus?'

Zac fought to control his anger. *Little boy?* But at the same time, his spy senses told him not to blow his cover. He couldn't risk being the centre of attention. He had to get that camera off him!

'Um, no,' he mumbled, looking down at his feet. 'I'm here because I really like, um … flowers.'

The presenter frowned, shrugged and moved on. 'What about you, little girl?' Zac heard him say. 'Frightened by the spinosaurus?'

Phew! Zac knew there was something off about the dinosaur, and he needed to keep moving if he was going to find Drastic. Operation Extinct was supposed to happen in just a few hours!

Zac walked away from the crowd and crept into the thick jungle. This whole place was a sort of like a laboratory – so where were all the scientists? They didn't seem to be inside the BioDome. Maybe they were underneath it.

And if so, that's probably where Dr Drastic was, too.

Zac snooped around, looking for any kind of hidden exit or tunnel. Soon he saw a hatch in the ground. He crept over and lifted the door open. Below was a ladder leading down into darkness.

Zac checked his SpyPad again. It was now 11.33 a.m. Less than two and a half hours to go. No time to lose!

Zac scurried down the ladder, which took him to a large room. There was a big roller door at one end and a doorway across the room.

Zac was about to sneak over when the roller door clanked open, revealing a ramp on the other side. He was clearly in some kind of delivery bay.

Two trucks backed down the ramp and into the bay. Zac ducked out of sight as the trucks came to a halt and men in overalls got out.

Zac noticed hundreds of tyre marks leading in and out of the bay. *So whatever these trucks are delivering,* he thought, *they're coming here all the time.*

Then Zac had a brainwave. Maybe they were delivering food for the spinosaurus! If it was a real dinosaur, it would need huge amounts of meat every day.

But the men weren't unloading meat. From one of the trucks, the men were carrying out little boxes with wires and knobs coming out of them.

They're not boxes, realised Zac. *They're batteries.* Suddenly he knew what was going on. The baby spinosaurus was obviously battery-powered – which meant it was a fake!

Zac felt a twinge of disappointment. *Leon will be upset,* he thought.

From the other truck, the men hooked up a hose and started pumping something into the ground. Zac sniffed the air. It smelt like when his mum filled the car up at the service station. Petrol!

Weird, thought Zac. *Why would Drastic need that much petrol?* He doubted that the spinosaurus was battery *and* petrol-powered.

The men climbed into the trucks. As the vehicles reversed up the ramp, BioDome staff dressed in white lab coats came in. They loaded the batteries onto trolleys and carted them out the door.

Zac counted to 20, then sprinted across the bay and slipped through after them.

The baby spinosaurus was fake, so Drastic obviously wasn't going to present his research to the International Science Council.

Maybe the petrol is part of Operation Extinct,

Zac realised. *What if Drastic is planning to drive a really big vehicle down to the Science Council HQ in Bladesville Central?*

Who knew what kind of crazy war machine Drastic could dream up?

I have to stop him! thought Zac.

Though the door, Zac found himself in a maze of white corridors.

Every so often, there was a door marked **STAFF ONLY** or **HAZARDOUS WASTE** or **LAB STORAGE**.

But Zac didn't have time to check every door. He had to follow his spy senses – and his senses told him he was getting closer and closer to Dr Drastic.

Suddenly, he heard a familiar voice from

behind him. 'Hello, Agent Rock Star.'

Zac spun around. As usual, his spy senses were right.

'Well, well,' sneered Dr Drastic. 'I wish I could say it was nice to see you again!'

CHAPTER

Dr Drastic was wearing a white lab coat, like the other BioDome staff, and had a name-tag pinned to his chest. There were two huge goons in grey jumpsuits behind him.

Dr Drastic stared at Zac with his icy blue eyes. Zac knew that one of those eyes was made of glass. It always creeped him out, but Zac never let it show.

'Congratulations on your fake baby dinosaur,' said Zac. 'Looks like it's inherited your good looks.'

Dr Drastic ignored him. 'I spotted you snooping around upstairs. I had the TV cameras bugged, you see. They're totally under my control – like everything in the BioDome. Including you!'

Zac only got as far as saying, 'You don't control me –' when Dr Drastic reached inside his lab coat and whipped out a strange device. It looked like a spray bottle of some kind.

Dr Drastic pointed the device at Zac and pulled a trigger on the handle.

Liquid shot from the nozzle straight at Zac!

SPLUUUURRT!

Before he could leap out of the way, Zac felt the thick spray hit his hands and face. He went to wipe the liquid away – then suddenly realised he couldn't move.

'A temporary muscle-constricting solution,' said Dr Drastic. 'I extracted it from a tropical plant that's been extinct for millions of years. The scientists here at the BioDome reconstructed its genetic sequence – with the help of my immense genius, of course.'

Zac went to talk, but even his jaw and tongue and facial muscles were stuck.

He was totally paralysed!

Dr Drastic clicked his fingers. Zac watched helplessly as the two goons stepped forward and picked him up. They hoisted Zac onto their shoulders and carted him down the winding maze of corridors.

Zac couldn't see where they were taking him. All he could do was stare up at the roof, and try to memorise the route they were following. He felt like he'd been turned into a statue.

Eventually he heard Dr Drastic's voice. 'Put him down over there.'

They'd left the twisting corridors and

were in a darker, more shadowy section of the complex. The henchmen planted Zac on his feet and leant him against a trolley.

They were inside what could only have been Dr Drastic's personal laboratory.

Zac had lost count of the number of times he'd been inside one of Drastic's labs. The evil scientist set them up everywhere, in volcanoes and diamond mines and underwater caves.

From the corner of his eye, Zac saw the two goons leave. Meanwhile, Dr Drastic gestured around the lab. He was holding some sort of remote control.

'Here's where it begins – Operation Extinct!' Dr Drastic boomed.

Then he gave Zac a concerned look. 'What's that, Rock Star? I can't quite hear you. It sounds like you're trying to tell me what a genius I am.'

Zac tried desperately to shake movement back into his muscles. The best he could do was wriggle his toes. Drastic had said the poison was temporary – so was it slowly wearing off?

Zac concentrated hard, trying to move a little more, and a little more, while Drastic chattered away.

'Well, you'd be right, I am a genius!' Dr Drastic grinned. 'And if you want further proof ...'

Drastic stabbed a button on his remote,

and a huge rectangular section of the laboratory floor slid away.

The smell of petrol hit Zac's nostrils. He saw steam rising up from the hole in the floor and heard a loud mechanical clanking from below.

If Zac hadn't been paralysed, his mouth would have dropped open for the second time that day. Because as the floor opened up, he realised that Drastic's baby spinosaurus had just been practice.

In the area beneath the floor, Drastic had built the biggest monster Zac had ever seen. It was a massive mechanical dinosaur, at least twenty times bigger than the baby spinosaurus upstairs.

So that's why Drastic needed all that petrol,
Zac gulped.

CHAPTER 7

'This is my masterpiece – the Robosaur!' crowed Dr Drastic. 'Remote-controlled and everything. Look, I can even make it blink!'

He pointed the remote at the enormous robosaur and clicked a button. Zac watched as sheets of metal folded over its glowing red LED eyes, and then opened again.

'It's so realistic,' bragged Dr Drastic. 'It mimics the act of blinking in a very natural way.'

Then the robosaur opened its mouth, and Zac got an all-too-clear glimpse of the jagged metal spikes Dr Drastic had used for its teeth.

Zac could still smell the stench of petrol, and he knew it must have an enormous engine somewhere inside.

I guess battery power wouldn't be enough for a robot dinosaur that big, he thought.

Zac tried to move his arms again. Movement had returned to his fingers, and he could turn his eyes from side to side.

The poison was wearing off, but would

it wear off fast enough for Zac to stop whatever Dr Drastic was planning? If he managed to stretch his arm out, he could use his SwingBands. But his hands were still pinned to his sides.

'I know you've guessed the truth about my baby dinosaur upstairs,' Dr Drastic was sneering. 'But not the whole truth. My experiment did work a little bit – I used the DNA sequence to research what a spinosaurus would look like, right down to the smallest detail. And then I hired the best animatronic makers in the business!'

Zac summoned all his energy. He still couldn't work his arms and legs, but at last he was able to get his jaw moving.

'Nothing – but – a fake,' Zac said through clenched teeth. 'Even Leon – can build – a robot!' Every word was a massive effort.

'You're missing the point, Rock Star,' ranted Drastic. 'I could have created the whole dinosaur out of living tissue, but the Science Council idiots wouldn't give me more money! They said it wasn't possible to bring a dinosaur back to life. Well, at two o'clock precisely, they're going to meet one face-to-face!'

So that's Operation Extinct, thought Zac. He had to keep this crazy scientist talking.

'I – suppose – you're going to let – that big thing – eat me?' he said.

'Don't be stupid,' snarled Dr Drastic, strolling over to a corner of the lab. He wheeled a turbo scooter out from behind a bench.

'This big thing, as you call it, is far more important than that. Together, we're going to tear down the Science Council Headquarters in Bladesville! Maybe *then* they'll reconsider funding my research!'

Yeah, sure, thought Zac. *They'll be so happy about you tearing their building down that they'll want to give you money, YOU CRAZY OLD MAN!*

Zac wanted to laugh, but it was no joke. People could get hurt. There were even GIB agents working undercover at the International Science Council, keeping an eye on all the latest scientific developments.

Dr Drastic had to be stopped!

'Anyway,' shouted Dr Drastic, stepping onto the turbo scooter, 'you're right about one thing.' He pressed a button on his remote control. 'You *are* going to be eaten!'

Zac heard a noise above him. He could move his neck muscles just enough to see three long green shapes slowly descending from the roof towards him.

At first he thought they were snakes. Then, to his relief, he realised they were jungle vines.

'Common liana crossed with a giant Venus flytrap,' shouted Dr Drastic, laughing madly. 'In other words, meat-eating vines! And they're attracted to heat, so you're a goner. So long, Agent Rock Star!'

Zac's relief suddenly vanished. The vines may as *well* have been snakes!

Drastic took his scooter into a small elevator in the wall of the lab, cackling madly as the doors slid shut.

Zac guessed that Drastic would ride alongside the robosaur, controlling it by remote all the way to the Science Council HQ.

But Zac had other problems to deal

with first. He was now alone in the lab with the meat-eating vines. And he still couldn't move his body!

CHAPTER

The hungry vines snaked closer and closer toward him. Zac could see their snapping, clam-like mouths and pointy, needle-sharp teeth ...

Suddenly, Zac remembered he'd been fitted with GIB issue MediMolars — fake teeth loaded with instant medication. All you had to do was prod the fake tooth three times with your tongue to open the tooth and release the medication. It would help Zac move again.

If only he'd remembered sooner! He felt like slapping himself in the head, except he was still paralysed.

Zac had two MediMolars. They were fitted right at the back of his bottom teeth, one on each side. One released an instant anti-toxin, designed to flush any poison from an agent's system.

The other MediMolar released an amnesia serum. If you were caught, it would make you temporarily forget everything you know — so you couldn't reveal GIB secrets under pressure.

The problem was, Zac couldn't quite remember which tooth did which. He was pretty sure it was the left tooth, but not 100 per cent ...

If I accidentally release the amnesia serum, I'll forget to open the other MediMolar, thought Zac. *I'll get eaten by the vines for sure!*

Zac decided to trust his gut instinct. He concentrated on using his tongue to prod the left MediMolar, just as the vines slithered down towards his head.

The MediMolar broke open, and Zac felt the medication flow through his body.

He flexed one hand, then the other. He could move! He raced out of the lab, just as the heat-seeking vines snapped down right where he'd been standing. He checked the time on his SpyPad as he ran.

It was 12.45 p.m. In just over an hour, Dr Drastic and his robosaur would be tearing down the International Science Council building.

Zac focused on the route he'd memorised when Dr Drastic's henchmen had carried him to the lab. When he was sure he had it clearly in his head, he sprinted off down the maze of corridors.

It took him almost 45 minutes, but eventually Zac bolted through the door into the delivery bay. He ran over to the ladder that led to the surface of the

BioDome and started climbing.

When he reached the top, he forced the door open and hauled himself up into the hot, dense jungle.

Zac fought his way through the vegetation towards the open spaces near the main door. When he came out, he was surprised to see that the crowds had gone. The place was empty.

Just as Zac remembered that the BioDome was closed to the public at one o'clock … three long green vines lashed out at him from the jungle!

More of Dr Drastic's meat-eating plants! Zac ducked and rolled, expertly dodging the vines' attack, then leapt to his feet and spun around.

This time he was ready. He reached into the pocket of his cargo pants and pulled out a spiky pinecone-shaped gadget with a black pin on the end.

It was an experimental GIB PhotoSynth Grenade. Guaranteed to distract people and animals with a burst of concentrated, artificial sunlight.

The meat-eating vines swung through the air for a moment, got a fix on Zac again, and flexed forward on their long, snake-like bodies.

Zac twisted the black pin on the gadget, setting the grenade's timer to five seconds. Then he pulled the pin and hurled the

grenade at the meat-eating vines.

FWOOOOSH!

There was a white flash. The vines stopped and reared up like cobras. They swayed in the air, dazzled by the light – giving Zac just enough time to slip away.

Zac pushed further and further through the jungle. He knew the main door was close. And then –

THUD!

Zac had run straight into something scaly and solid. The impact knocked him on his back.

He looked up to see the giant baby spinosaurus standing above him. Unlike Zac, the dinosaur had managed to remain on its feet. It had hardly budged when Zac ran into it.

Zac backed away, trying not to panic. It was just a robot, but Drastic had probably programmed it with all the speed and hunting skills of a real spinosaurus.

And it also happened to be blocking the only door to the outside.

CHAPTER

Zac ran through a list of tactics in his mind. *I can't outrun it,* he thought. Could he trick it? Offer it some instant SpyFood? Confuse it with a blast of Axe Grinder from his music collection?

Think, Zac! he told himself.

And then he realised something. The robot spinosaurus wasn't moving *at all*.

Of course, thought Zac, as he got to his feet. If the baby spinosaurus was battery-powered, Drastic would switch it off when no-one was around.

Relieved, Zac checked the time. It was 1.37 p.m. Just 22 minutes left to save the day!

He raced through the main doors of the BioDome and out into the streets of Bladesville. In the distance he could hear yelling, and hundreds of car horns honking and blaring. It sounded to Zac like Drastic had taken his giant robosaur to the street.

As Zac ran, a plan popped into his head. He switched on his SwingBands, hoping madly that they still had power in them.

He focused on a building up ahead and blinked. An instant later, he was suddenly pulled through the air.

WHOOSH!

Zac swung from building to building, following the trail of damage Dr Drastic and his robosaur had left behind.

Aim, blink,

WHOOSH!

Aim, blink,

WHOOSH!

Zac wondered if he'd get a warning when the SwingBands' power was running out. Leon was useless at adding important features like that.

Zac looked down as he rushed past

the street below. There were squashed vehicles everywhere. Luckily it looked like everyone had got out and run for cover when they'd seen the giant metal monster coming.

Dr Drastic would be heading straight for Bladesville Central. Zac was sure to catch sight of him any moment now ... *There!*

Up ahead, Zac saw the robot dinosaur stomping straight towards the International Science Council building. He could just make out Dr Drastic riding alongside on his turbo scooter.

The robosaur was enormous. Along its spine was the same sort of fin the baby spinosaurus had on its back, except the robot dinosaur's fin was made of thin, flexible metal. Drastic clearly hadn't bothered to make this one look completely real.

Zac had to bring down the robosaur before it reached the Council's building and really went crazy. He only had one plan, and he just had to hope it worked ...

Zac swung closer and closer, and when he was near enough, he pointed his hand at the robosaur's back and blinked.

ZAP! SHOOOOONK!

The SwingBands locked him on. Zac was flying straight towards the robosaur!

Just before he slammed into the

creature's metal body, Zac reached out and grabbed hold of the fin. He clung tight to the flexible sheet of metal, which bent and wobbled as the robosaur crunched its way into Main Square.

Luckily, Drastic hadn't seen him yet.

Zac used his hands to edge himself closer to the robosaur's head. Soon he was at the base of its neck. Zac let go of the fin, balanced himself on his hands and feet, then pulled himself up towards the head.

Zac was very, very careful not to blink – his SwingBands were still powered on and he didn't want to go flying off the robosaur before he could stop it.

Down on the ground, Dr Drastic

whooped with delight, unaware that Zac was on the robosaur.

Zac slowly pulled the SwingBands from his hands and unpeeled the suction pad from the back of his neck. He reached out to the head of the robosaur – but at that exact moment, the crazy scientist looked up and saw Zac!

'Noooooo!' he screamed.

Zac moved quickly, strapping the SwingBands onto the robosaur's head and planting the suction pad just near the glowing LED eyes. He desperately hoped his plan would work!

Dr Drastic sneered. 'I know what you're trying to do, Rock Star,' he yelled.

'You think you can turn off its Cybernetic brain! Well, forget it – you'll never get through that metal plating!'

'You'll see,' smiled Zac. 'Whoops, better watch out!'

Zac pointed ahead. The robot dinosaur was about to crash into a huge flashing billboard. Dr Drastic panicked and fumbled with his remote control – madly pressing buttons as he tried to steer the robot dinosaur away from the billboard.

Zac clung to the creature's neck. He had to jump off, because any second now, the robosaur was going to blink.

And when he did –

WHOOOOOOSH!

Suddenly Zac felt the robosaur get whisked upwards. The giant mechanical monster had blinked, and locked the SwingBands onto a nearby building – and now it was flying through the air!

CHAPTER 10

Gotta go, thought Zac. Taking a deep breath, he flung himself off the robosaur ...

... And then he was flying through the air without SwingBands. And no way to land safely!

Suddenly Zac had an idea.

He pulled the SafeCrate from his pocket and expanded it to full size as he fell.

With just seconds before he slammed into the ground, Zac pulled himself inside the SafeCrate and slammed the door shut.

He pressed his hands and feet against the walls as –

BOING!!!!!

The SafeCrate hit the ground. Zac stretched out like a starfish, trying to stay limp as the impact sent shockwaves through his body.

He felt the SafeCrate bounce, bounce, bounce – and then gently roll to a stop.

Zac leapt out of the SafeCrate as fast as he could. He needed to see what had happened!

The whole of Main Square was buzzing

with choppers, but the giant robosaur was nowhere to be found.

Then Zac saw it – the smoking, mangled wreck of the robot dinosaur, wedged in an alley between two buildings.

But where was Dr Drastic? He was gone!

That lousy scientist! thought Zac, clenching his fists.

He was glad everyone was safe from the robosaur, but he was annoyed that Drastic had gotten away.

One of the GIB choppers landed in the middle of Main Square, and Leon jumped out.

'Zac!' he called. 'We've been trying to

get you on your SpyPad!'

'Sorry, Leon,' said Zac. 'I was a bit busy bringing down a monster robosaur!'

'I know,' said Leon. 'We saw the whole thing. Quick thinking with the SwingBands, by the way. I'm amazed they worked on the robosaur – they're only designed for human brains.'

'Well,' said Zac smugly, 'the brain *is* just a big computer, after all.'

Leon nodded. 'That is so right.'

Zac rolled his eyes. 'Hey, by the way – how are you going to cover up a giant robot dinosaur attacking Bladesville?'

'Don't worry, GIB has it sorted,' Leon said. 'Our undercover agents are telling the papers that it's a runaway prop from the new *Killer Robots* movie.'

Zac laughed. People would believe anything! Just then, he felt his SpyPad vibrating. He had an incoming message from his mum.

Good work on Operation Extinct, said the message. *But don't forget you've got Operation Compost when you get home!*

TOMB OF DOOM

CHAPTER 1

Sometimes, thought Zac Power, *being a spy isn't as cool as it sounds.*

Right now he was on a camel in the middle of the desert. Zac knew that this might sound good to another kid. But it really wasn't.

For one thing Zac's camel kept spitting gross stuff onto his sneakers. Then there was the heat. The sand was so hot that if you were dumb enough to walk on it without shoes your feet would melt up to your ankles — just like butter on hot toast.

The heat was terrible for Zac's hair, too. He had already used half a tube of Super-Strength Hair Gel.

The other reason this trip wasn't cool was that his entire family was here too. Everyone in the Power family was a spy, even Zac's geeky brother Leon.

They all worked for the Government Investigation Bureau, or GIB for short. Zac had been on some awesome missions, but this family holiday wasn't one of them.

Zac tried to pass the time by playing the latest game on his SpyPad.

Zac's SpyPad was a super high-tech mini-tablet with a mobile satellite phone, a laser and a code-breaker.

Zac was usually excellent at electronic games, but this one had him stumped.

It was called *Pyramid Panic*. Whenever he reached the treasure room in the middle of the pyramid he was ejected out through a hole in the roof. Zac's highest score so far was 2000. One player called A.T.S. had the top score of 200,000! *Dumb game,* thought Zac, as he deleted it from his SpyPad.

The tour guide on the front camel was droning on.

'We are now entering the desert region

of the Amber Sands. The famous Vanishing Pyramid which is the tomb of the Golden Sun King is said to be located here,' he said. 'It's the only pyramid never to be looted by tomb raiders.'

'That's because it's guarded by GIB,' Leon whispered to Zac. 'Apparently it's stuffed full of treasure.'

'According to legend,' continued the guide, 'if the Vanishing Pyramid is ever broken into terrible earthquakes will shake the Amber Sands. The locals call the pyramid the Tomb of Doom …'

As he spoke something really strange happened. The earth began to tremble.

RRRRRRRUMBLE!

The tour guide went pale.

'Let's all stop here,' he said nervously. But Zac's camel wouldn't stop. With a snort it turned and galloped away from the group.

'Bye, sweetie!' called his mum. 'Don't forget to wear your hat!'

The camel galloped faster and faster. And faster. And *faster!* It went so fast that smoke started streaming out of its nose.

Smoke? thought Zac. *That can't be right…*

Then he noticed a metal plate attached to the camel's neck, hidden by fur.

CAMELTRONIC 9000.

Zac had heard about the this from Leon. It was a state-of-the-art robot with ten gears and airbags. Zac wished he'd realised this earlier – the CAMELTRONIC had a drinks dispenser in its hump!

Had GIB arranged for this camel to take him to his next mission? There was nothing Zac could do but wait and see …

On and on the camel ran until finally they reached an oasis. The camel groaned and collapsed in a heap beneath a palm tree. Zac quickly jumped off and looked around. There was nothing there except a pond and the palm tree.

Zac had been hoping that he was about to be sent on some cool mission. But that was clearly a false alarm. Disappointed, Zac kicked the palm tree.

'Stop that,' said the tree, crossly.

Zac looked closer and saw that the tree was actually GIB Agent Peterson in disguise. Agent Peterson shook one of his leaves and a date fell onto the sand.

'Eat that,' he commanded.

Zac bit carefully into the soft flesh. He normally didn't like dates, but he suspected that this wasn't a normal date. Sure enough, his teeth hit something hard. Zac spat out a metal disk.

All right! His next mission! It had been ages since Zac had gone on a mission.

Sure beats this boring family holiday, he thought.

Zac loaded the disk into his SpyPad.

...loading...

CLASSIFIED
MISSION INITIATED: 2 P.M.

Top GIB spy, Agent Track Starr, is MIA while guarding the Vanishing Pyramid. Tremors have rocked the Amber Sands region, which means the pyramid has been entered. Raiders may have broken into the tomb, and GIB now fears Agent Track Star is trapped inside.

YOUR MISSION
- Locate and enter the Vanishing Pyramid
- Find and/or rescue Agent Track Star
- Repair any damage done to the pyramid

SPECIAL NOTE
If anyone remains inside the Vanishing Pyramid 24 hours after tremors first start, the pyramid will collapse. Anyone inside will be trapped forever!
END

Just then, the ground shook again.

Zac turned to Agent Peterson.

'When did these tremors start?' he asked urgently.

'About two hours ago,' replied Agent Peterson. 'Just after Agent Track Star went missing.'

Right. Zac knew he had to click into action. He looked at his SpyPad.

2.00 P.M.

If Agent Track Star had already been inside the pyramid for two hours, that meant he had until midday tomorrow ...

Zac was already behind time!

CHAPTER 2

Zac wanted to set off straight away. But there was one small problem. The CAMELTRONIC 9000 was in no state to go anywhere.

Luckily Agent Peterson seemed to know exactly what Zac was thinking. He shook his leaves again and a set of keys fell into Zac's hands.

At first Zac didn't know what the keys were for. Then he spotted a cool looking car behind Agent Peterson.

It was a buggy that was painted bright green. It had a roll bar instead of a roof and on the back was a big solar panel.

Awesome! A solar-powered dune buggy!

Zac jumped in and started it up.

'There's a Pyramid-Pack in the back that Agent Tech Head put together for you,' said Agent Peterson. 'It's full of useful gadgets for a mission like this.'

'Great,' said Zac. 'Now, which way do I go?'

'North, I think,' replied Agent Peterson. 'Or maybe east.' He didn't sound very sure.

I'll head north-east, decided Zac as he revved the engine and set off. It was strange not having proper directions but Zac wasn't worried. Surely it couldn't hurt to go for a short joy-ride first!

The dune buggy was excellent. It zipped around palm trees and screeched around boulders. Zac even drove it on two wheels. Then he flew over the sand dunes, making huge sand clouds behind him as he bounced back down on the big fat tyres.

After a while, Zac started getting hungry. Was there any food in the buggy? Zac couldn't find any. But then he noticed a button on the dashboard with a picture of a hamburger on it.

Curiously, Zac pushed it. With a whirr the buggy's bonnet folded up. Underneath was a barbecue grill.

As Zac watched, a mechanical arm slapped a meat patty onto the sizzling grill while another arm chopped up lettuce and tomatoes. Ten minutes later Zac was eating a delicious burger. There were even some chips on the side.

The dune buggy's clock beeped.

4.00 P.M.

He'd been on this mission for two hours and didn't even know where he was heading yet. Time to talk to Agent Tech Head.

'Hi, Leon,' said Zac when his brother's face appeared in the SpyPad's screen.

'Any idea where to find this Tomb of Doom?'

'I haven't been able to find the exact location,' Leon admitted, 'but I'll send you what I know. There are some sunglasses in the Pyramid-Pack. Put them on.'

The sunglasses were much less cool-looking than the ones Zac was already wearing. But when he put on them on he understood why Leon wanted him to wear them.

Head Up Display sunglasses!

Any information Leon sent was beamed directly onto the inside of each lens.

Leon sent through a message straight away.

The Vanishing Pyramid is located somewhere around 27.66⁰ latitude and 28.25⁰ longitude.

Zac entered the coordinates into the SpyPad's GPS. Then Leon sent another message.

Don't believe everything you see.

What did that mean?

But there was no time to wonder. Zac had to keep going. He found his favourite driving music on his SpyPad: Axe Grinder's *Get Loud*. Then he slipped the buggy into cruise control and settled back. He still had a long way to drive.

The sun was setting when Zac finally spotted a building on the horizon. That *had* to be the Vanishing Pyramid! Zac jammed his foot on the accelerator. But instead of speeding up, the dune buggy slowed down and then stopped altogether.

Zac looked at the battery meter and groaned. He was out of solar power! He was going to have to make the rest of the journey on foot.

Even though it was evening the sand was still burning hot. When Zac tested it with the tip of his sneaker it instantly started turning into goo. There was no way Zac could walk across here!

Quickly he checked the Pyramid-Pack.

In it he found a pair of daggy sandals and some white knee-high socks. Zac put the socks back straight away. There was *no way* he was wearing socks and sandals. That was something Leon would do!

But Zac took a closer look at the sandals. They were Track Changers. A dial on the side of each shoe allowed him to choose what kind of animal prints he wanted them to make.

Zac didn't need to disguise his foot-prints but he slipped the shoes on anyway. He remembered from spy training that Track Changers were heat-proof!

Zac chose 'Camel' and headed towards the Vanishing Pyramid.

CHAPTER 3

Zac trudged through the moonlight for what felt like hours until the pyramid was just up ahead. And then the Vanishing Pyramid ... vanished!

'Woah!' said Zac. 'Where did it go?' He spun around and there it was behind him. Zac ran towards it. But when he got close the pyramid disappeared again. It reappeared a few moments later in a new spot. Then Zac remembered Leon's final message: *Don't believe everything you see.*

Could there be some kind of mirage generator protecting the pyramid? Zac knew that mirages often looked so real that people imagined they could see water when there was nothing but hot air. Perhaps that was what was happening now.

Zac needed a way of telling the difference between the real and the imaginary. Then he remembered the latest app that he had downloaded for his SpyPad: the Mirage Filter.

He switched the Mirage Filter app on. When he held it up to the pyramid that kept disappearing, there was nothing on the screen. This meant that the pyramid was a mirage.

Then Zac scanned around the desert and a pyramid appeared clearly on the screen in area where there was nothing to see at all. Zac smiled. That had to be the real Vanishing Pyramid!

Zac checked his SpyPad. **8.32 P.M.**

He'd wasted a lot of time chasing mirages. Better get moving.

Zac raced towards the true location of the Vanishing Pyramid. At first he couldn't see anything. But as he got closer, the Vanishing Pyramid began to appear, like it was coming out of a fog.

The closer Zac got the more solid it became. Finally the pyramid was right in front of him. Zac reached out his hand. It was a big relief to feel the solid rock beneath his fingers.

But now Zac faced a new problem.

How do I get in there?

He walked around the outside looking for clues. Halfway around he saw some hieroglyphics and his spy senses started tingling. Maybe this would tell him how to get in.

Zac had a pretty good idea what the symbols might mean. But just to be sure he switched his SpyPad into Code-Breaking mode and scanned it along the rock.

Seconds later, the SpyPad flashed the decoded message up on screen.

Knock before entering.

Could it be that simple to get into the pyramid? It didn't seem possible.

Well, it can't hurt to try, thought Zac. He rapped sharply on the rock.

Instantly it slid away to reveal a dark cavern. Zac stepped inside. With a thud the rock slid back into place and Zac found himself in total darkness. Time to switch the SpyPad into Glow mode.

Once he had some light Zac looked around. What he saw took his breath away. The walls around him were covered in paintings. One painting showed a room full of glittering jewels. Another painting was of enormous snakes. There was also a painting of people being chased by huge scorpions.

In front of Zac were three golden doorways, each decorated with precious stones. Behind them were three tunnels leading off into the darkness. He was at the start of a maze!

Agent Track Star must have gone down one of these, thought Zac. *But which one?*

Zac knew that lots of pyramids were filled with booby traps and false passages.

Were the paintings a warning of what lay ahead? Zac didn't like the look of the snakes or the scorpions.

Which way should he go?

CHAPTER

4

Better speak to Leon again, decided Zac. But the thick walls of the pyramid made it hard to get a clear signal. Leon's face appeared fuzzy on the screen of his SpyPad and his voice kept dropping out.

'Play the game,' was all that Zac could hear. It wasn't like Leon to talk about games during a mission.

'*Pyramid Panic*,' Leon finally yelled before the signal dropped out.

Pyramid Panic? That stupid game that Zac had deleted from his SpyPad? Why was Leon telling him to play that when he wanted help through this maze?

Hang on, thought Zac. *The maze in* Pyramid Panic *must be the same as the one inside the Vanishing Pyramid!*

The more he thought about it the more sense it made. GIB probably made the game to disguise what they knew about the inside of the Vanishing Pyramid. That way if a SpyPad ever fell into enemy hands they wouldn't realise what the game really was.

It was a clever idea. But there was one

slight problem. Zac didn't have the game any more. He was going to have to rely on what he could remember.

Zac looked at the three entrances and thought about the last time he'd played *Pyramid Panic*. The left-hand passage led to a dead end. And he was pretty sure the right-hand one ended up in a deep hole. He knew that because he'd fallen into it a couple of times.

Easy! That only left the middle passage.

As he headed into the dark tunnel Zac saw something scratched into the ground.

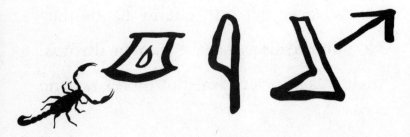

Zac smiled — he didn't need his SpyPad to solve this clue.

His school project on Egypt had taught him enough to work out the letters …

G I B

My hunch was right, he thought. *Agent Track Star must have gone this way!*

Just then the ground rumbled and the walls shook. Zac set off again at a brisk pace. There was no way he was getting stuck in here!

After walking for hours Zac stopped to check the time.

11.15 P.M.

This didn't feel like the right way any more. *I'll keep going for a bit longer*, Zac thought, taking a step forward. And then the ground disappeared!

Zac plunged into a deep hole. As he landed his head whacked against the side of the hole.

Instantly, Zac was knocked out.

He wasn't sure how much time had passed when he finally came round. But losing any time at all was bad. *Great*, Zac thought, annoyed. *How do I get out?*

It was very dark in the hole. He felt around for his SpyPad to get some light. But it wasn't there! He must have dropped it in the passage above when he fell.

This was just like playing *Pyramid Panic*, but worse. At least with the game he could turn it off and start all over again when things went bad.

Zac felt the walls around him. They were very slippery and steep. If only he had some sort of light! It was impossible to do anything in this darkness.

Zac looked down and saw a bluish light moving around the floor. He blinked a few times but the light was still there. A moment later it was joined by other blue lights. Soon there were enough lights for Zac to see what was going on.

The crawling lights were beetles with big horns. Each one was the size of Zac's palm and had wings that glowed with a purple light. They looked familiar to Zac, but where from?

Oh yeah! Ultraviolet Glowing Scarab Beetles – Zac had seen them on Leon's favourite nature show – *Creepy Creatures*.

Then Zac had a brilliant idea. He fished out the ugly knee-high socks from the Pyramid-Pack. Then he carefully scooped up the beetles and put them in the sock.

Before long the sock was glowing as brightly as a torch. The beetles wriggled a lot but Zac tied a knot in the end so they couldn't escape.

Don't worry, he promised them. *I'll let you*

go later. Then he held up the sock-torch to have a look around.

On the side of the hole he saw another carving:

This was nothing that he'd learnt at school and he didn't have his SpyPad decoder with him. *I'll just have to work it out for myself*, Zac realised.

He looked carefully at the pictures. The first one was obviously a door. The second one was a figure with its finger to its lips – it looked like his mum when she wanted him to be quiet or when something was a secret. *Maybe there's a secret exit around here?* thought Zac.

Zac shone the torch around and there in the ground was a small hook. He pulled it, and instantly a rock slid back in the wall to reveal a passage leading up. It was very narrow.

Zac would have to wriggle through it on his stomach. And what if it didn't lead back up to the main passage?

But Zac knew this was probably the only way out of this hole. He was going to have to just risk it.

CHAPTER 5

Zac started wriggling up the passage. It was a tight squeeze and he couldn't see any light ahead. But the tunnel was sloping upwards and it wasn't long before he climbed back into the main passageway.

His SpyPad was on the ground near the edge of the hole. Zac grabbed it and checked the time.

It was already dawn and he was no closer to finding Agent Track Star. Suddenly, the ground trembled again. Zac covered his head as pebbles pelted down. They were becoming stronger. Zac had to hurry!

Zac tied his beetle-torch to his Pyramid-Pack as he hurried along. Ahead of him the corridor went off in two different directions. *Which way should I go?* There was no way he wanted to end up down another hole.

Then Zac saw something out of the corner of his eye. There was writing on the floor of the left-hand passage.

He shone the SpyPad's glowing screen at the spot but the word instantly vanished. Zac was puzzled for a moment. Then he had an idea. *Maybe whatever it is can only be seen with ultraviolet light.*

Zac shone the beetle-torch over the ground. Sure enough, stamped on the ground, was 'GIB'! *Agent Track Star must have used the GIB Invisible Stamp-pad to leave a clue!* It was a way for GIB agents to leave secret messages for each other.

Usually Zac had to turn on the ultraviolet screen in his SpyPad to see the invisible ink. But the beetle-torch was doing the same job. *Agent Track Star definitely came this way,* thought Zac. *I must be on the right track.*

Zac shone the beetle-torch down the left-hand tunnel. More glowing marks appeared, leading all the way down.

This mission just got a whole lot easier, chuckled Zac.

He followed the marks for a while but then, quite suddenly, they stopped. The tunnel ended at the doorway of a small room. Zac looked in. On the back wall was a giant painting of a human with a cat's head. Zac took a step backwards. He was more of a dog person than a cat person. And there was something *very* dodgy about this cat.

Zac knew that a spy must always trust his gut instincts. He picked up a rock and rolled it into the middle of the room.

ZZZZAAAAP!

A zap of light shot out of the cat's eye and blasted the pebble into a pile of dust.

Being careful not to step any further into the room Zac held up his torch and took a better look at the painting. Over the cat's eye was something that looked like a glass marble cut in half.

An ancient magnifying lens! thought Zac.

He was pretty sure he knew what was going on. But he wanted to check. He rolled another rock into the room and watched.

When the rock fell into the cat's path a lever behind its eye flipped up. This allowed a ray of sunlight to come through a hole behind the eye. When the sunbeam hit the magnifying glass, it acted like a laser beam. Anything that crossed its path would be instantly destroyed.

Zac was impressed. Of course, during the night it wouldn't work at all. But during daylight it was deadly.

Zac couldn't resist trying the laser out one more time. He took off his hat. It was the one his mum always made him wear in the sun. It was totally ugly and scratchy too. Zac flicked the hat into the room.

PFFFFT!

It disappeared into a puff of smoke.

Excellent!

After seeing the rocks and the hat blasted away there was no way Zac was going to risk walking in there. He needed a way of covering the cat's eye.

Zac felt in his pocket. He had a couple of paint bombs that would do the trick. But they would also wreck the wall-paintings and he didn't really want to do that. The paintings were old and faded but they were kind of cool too. Plus his mission was to *repair* the damage in the pyramid, not make more.

So Zac pulled out some chewing gum and a rubber band instead. Perfect! Zac quickly chewed the gum into a ball and then flicked it across the room with the rubber band.

KERRR-SPLAT!

Bullseye! The gum was now covering the magnifying lens.

But Zac didn't have time to feel pleased with himself.

Every second counted.

He had to keep moving.

CHAPTER

Zac quickly walked through the Cat Room and out another door on the far wall. The passage continued for a bit and then Zac found himself in another room.

Cool! The Mummy Room.

Lying on a table in the middle of the room was a golden sarcophagus. Zac knew that this was a kind of coffin mummies were kept in.

The room was cold. And really dark. In fact, it was kind of creepy. But Zac wasn't the type of kid who got scared. He especially wasn't the type to be scared of some old, dead mummy.

Suddenly Zac heard a banging noise. It was coming from inside the sarcophagus! Most kids would probably have run away screaming at this point. But not Zac. *There must be a simple explanation,* he thought. *I'll just open up the sarcophagus and see what's inside.* But all the same his heart was beating hard as he walked towards the noise.

CREEEEEEEEEAK!

The sarcophagus was very heavy to open. Inside was a figure about the same height as Zac, wrapped in bandages.

Its arms rose up like a zombie, and it moaned as it came towards him.

It can't really be a mummy, thought Zac. *I need to get those bandages off and see what — or who — is underneath.*

He reached into the Pyramid-Pack and his hand closed around something that felt like a can of fly spray. That wouldn't be much use. Zac checked the label. *Bandage-B-Gone,* it said. *Super strength instant bandage remover.* Leon had thought of everything when he put this Pyramid-Pack together!

Just as the mummy lurched towards him, Zac sprayed the figure with the Bandage-B-Gone.

A massive cloud instantly billowed up in the air as the bandages dissolved. Zac heard coughing coming from inside the cloud.

'Who's there?' he asked, sharply. 'Show yourself.'

'It's Agent Track Star,' came the reply. Zac was puzzled. Agent Track Star didn't sound how he was expecting him to.

When the cloud cleared Zac gasped at what he saw. He now knew why Agent Track Star sounded different.

Agent Track Star was a girl!

'I got caught in a booby trap,' explained Agent Track Star when she stopped coughing. 'One minute I was walking along and the next thing I knew I was wrapped up in bandages inside that sarcophagus. Thanks for rescuing me. You must be Zac Power. I'm Caz.'

Zac looked at her suspiciously.

'What are you doing in here anyway? You were supposed to be guarding the pyramid from the outside,' he said.

'I thought I heard tomb raiders inside,' replied Caz. 'I decided to go in and save the Golden Sun Diamond.'

Suddenly Caz's eyes filled with tears. For a horrible moment Zac thought she might cry.

'But I can't do it on my own,' she said. 'I need help.'

'I'll help you,' said Zac. 'We're both GIB agents after all. We're *supposed* to help each other.' Caz smiled gratefully.

'Cool. Follow me,' she said. And she took off down a corridor.

Zac had little choice but to follow her. There wasn't much time left.

8.54 P.M.

He hoped Caz knew what she was doing. She led him down winding passageways and in and out of rooms, all at a really fast pace.

'You know your way around here pretty well,' Zac said. He was getting puffed trying to keep up.

'I'm the top scorer on *Pyramid Panic*,' said Caz proudly. 'I know this place backwards.'

Finally Caz stopped.

'This is the Treasure Room,' she said.

Zac gasped. Around the walls were piles of gold coins and sparkling jewels. Right in the middle was a giant statue with a lion's head. And in its hands was the biggest jewel Zac had ever seen. It was easily the size of a basketball.

'The statue is the Golden Sun King,' whispered Caz. 'And in his lap is the Golden Sun Diamond.'

'It's amazing it's never been stolen,' said Zac. Caz nodded.

'Yep, apparently there's some curse protecting it,' she said. 'It's meant to be guarded by a huge army of scorpions...'

Just then, the floor rumbled again.

RRRRRUMBLE!

This time it wasn't just pebbles that fell from the ceiling. It was rocks the size of Zac's fist! It felt like the pyramid was beginning to collapse.

'We've got to leave,' yelled Zac above the noise.

'No!' yelled back Caz. 'The diamond isn't safe in here. We have to take it back to Headquarters.'

Zac looked at Caz. Although she was supposed to be a top spy she seemed like a little kid to Zac. *She doesn't even look strong enough to lift that diamond*, thought Zac. But she also seemed pretty stubborn.

He could tell there was no way she was leaving without it.

'Let me get it,' Zac said, taking a step towards the statue.

Caz grabbed his arm.

'Look out!' she cried, pointing down-wards. In front of Zac was a wide trench. Out of it was coming a strange hissing sound. Then a giant cobra, thicker than Zac's leg, rose up out of the trench. It stared at him with its black, beady eyes.

Seconds later another one appeared beside it.

Then another.

And another.

CHAPTER 7

Zac stood very still. He knew that the slightest movement would cause the cobras to strike. But the snakes hadn't seen Caz. She was hidden behind Zac.

'Caz,' Zac whispered. 'Get my SpyPad out of my Pyramid-Pack.' He felt Caz reach into the Pyramid-Pack and pull it out.

'Now, find the album *Music for Soothing Savage Beasts* and put it on speaker.'

'Which song?' whispered Caz.

'Track seven,' Zac replied. At least he *hoped* it was track seven. He held his breath.

For a terrible moment he thought the SpyPad's batteries had gone flat. But then the track started.

Phew! It was the right track after all: 'Snake Charming Song'. The moment the cobras heard the music they began swaying backwards and forwards, like fans at a rock concert.

'Nice work, Zac!' said Caz, looking impressed. 'Now, grab the diamond.'

Zac jumped across the cobra pit. The snakes paid no attention to him at all.

He reached out to pick up the diamond.

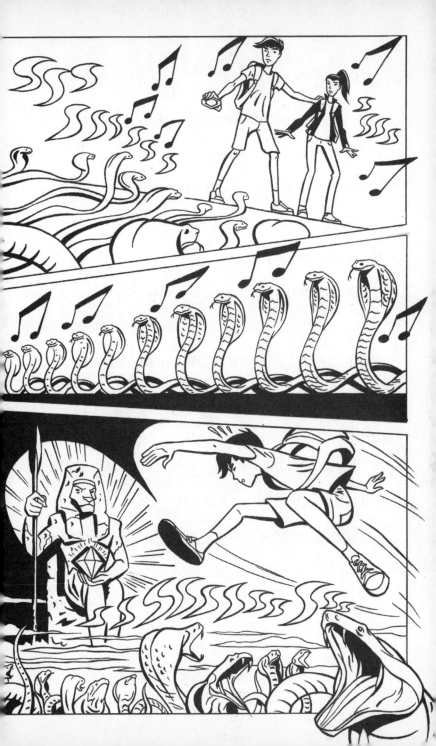

But then he stopped. He remembered what Caz had said about the curse. He didn't believe in that stuff, of course. All the same though, he couldn't help feeling that something wasn't right. But there was no time to worry about it.

Zac grabbed the diamond. Underneath was a big dark hole. Zac froze, waiting for something to happen. But nothing did. Zac relaxed. The curse was obviously just made up to scare people.

'Caz,' called Zac. 'I can't jump across the pit with this – I'm going to throw the diamond across. Do you think you can catch it?'

Caz nodded. So Zac threw the diamond.

To his surprise Caz had no trouble catching it. In fact, she caught it with one hand and then twirled it on one finger. Then she shoved the diamond in her backpack.

'Thanks Zac,' she grinned. 'I'm off to HQ.'

'Hang on,' said Zac. 'We can go there together.'

Caz seemed different all of a sudden. She laughed. It was a nasty laugh.

'Oh, I'm not going to GIB's HQ,' she said. 'I work for BIG now. And I'm going to get a massive promotion when I come back with this diamond. Thanks for helping me steal it.'

BIG! Zac had heard about them. They

were the most evil and devious spies in the business. Now it all made sense.

'You're a double agent!' exclaimed Zac.

'That's right,' smiled Caz. 'I've been pretending to work for GIB while all along I was spying for BIG. Well Zac, it's been fun but now I'm going to have to leave you alone with these snakes.'

'But I rescued you from the sarcophagus!' said Zac angrily. 'You'd still be stuck in there if I hadn't come along!'

'You didn't rescue me,' Caz sneered. 'I didn't become the top player on *Pyramid Panic* without learning where all the booby traps are! I only pretended to be trapped so you would feel sorry for me and help me steal the diamond. Why should *I* do the dangerous work when I could trick you into doing it instead?'

Zac stared at Caz in shock. He couldn't believe anyone could be so devious.

'Bye, Zac Power!' said Caz, as she turned and ran towards the door. 'You're not a bad spy. You're *almost* as good as me. Maybe you should join BIG too?'

'I'd never work for BIG,' said Zac angrily.

'That's too bad,' said Caz, stopping at the door and shrugging. 'See you later, *loser!*'

Zac checked the time.

11.39 A.M.

Things were going terribly wrong.

Caz was escaping with the Golden Sun Diamond and Zac knew it wouldn't be long before his SpyPad went flat.

When the music stopped those cobras were going to attack him for sure. And then things got even worse.

Zac heard a low, rumbling sound.

At first he thought it was another earth tremor. But then he realised the sound was coming from the hole that the diamond had been covering!

In shock Zac watched as a giant scorpion scuttled out of the hole. It was twice the size of his hand! Another scorpion followed behind the first. And another.

Then hundreds of scorpions came

flooding out, like water from a burst pipe. Zac couldn't help noticing that their tails were already up in the sting position. And they were heading straight for him.

CHAPTER 8

Zac tried to leap out of the way. But he was too late. The scorpions swarmed all over him. So Zac stood very still, hoping that they would think he was a rock.

The scorpions ran under his clothes and over his face. Their legs were very ticklish, but Zac didn't feel like laughing. *It's only a matter of time before I get stung,* he thought.

He just hoped there was some anti-venom in the Pyramid-Pack. But to his amazement the scorpions ran right over him and out the door.

They're chasing Caz! realised Zac. *They know she's got the diamond!*

What should he do? *I could just wait until the scorpions catch her,* thought Zac. There was no way she could outrun that many angry, giant scorpions. The other option was to rescue her. If he did then she would have to admit that *he* was the better spy. And she'd have to apologise for calling him a loser!

Zac liked that idea. But how was he going to rescue her?

He checked his Track Changer sandals.

Maybe there was an animal on that dial that could help him out.

Fox? No good.

Coyote? Nup.

Kangaroo? Bingo!

He switched the shoes to 'Kangaroo' and took an enormous jump.

SPRRRROOOOOIIIING!

Zac leapt straight over the snake pit and took off down the passageway. It wasn't long before he could see Caz up ahead. She was running fast, but the scorpions were catching up.

Zac jumped as hard as he could. Soon he was right behind the scorpions. Zac bent his knees. This next jump was going to have to be the biggest one he'd ever done.

SPRRRROOOOOIIIING!

With an enormous jump Zac leapt over the swarm of scorpions and landed right behind Caz. He reached out and grabbed her backpack firmly in his hand. She jerked to a halt as he turned and jumped back over the scorpions.

'Hey!' yelled Caz angrily as she found herself pulled backwards through the air. 'What are you doing?'

'I'm rescuing you,' replied Zac. 'We have to return the diamond or you'll be stung by those scorpions.'

'There's no way I'm being rescued by you, Zac Power!' snarled Caz.

Still in mid-air she wiggled her arms out of the backpack and fell to the ground in a commando roll. She landed right in the path of the scorpions. But they scuttled right over the top of her without even stopping. They were after the bag with the diamond in it. And the bag was now in Zac's hand!

The walls began to shake again. They shook so much it was like the pyramid had suddenly been turned into jelly.

'Forget the diamond!' yelled Caz. 'This place is about to collapse. I'm outta here!' Then she ran off into the darkness.

Zac checked his SpyPad as he bounced back towards the statue.

There was no time to chase Caz now. As much as he hated to do it, he would have to let her escape. He had to stick to his mission now and return the diamond.

Anyway, he had a feeling they would meet again.

CHAPTER

The scorpions were close behind ... and were getting closer with every second! But Zac managed to stay just ahead of them.

A few bounces later he was back in the Treasure Room. Zac opened Caz's bag and yanked out the diamond. The statue was still a couple of leaps away, and the scorpions were closer than ever.

Zac skidded to a halt.

Blocking his path was the trench.

The cobras!

The SpyPad had stopped playing and one look at the snakes told Zac that they were no longer in a trance. In fact, they looked nastier than ever.

Zac thought fast. *I'll have to throw the diamond back over the snake pit and into the statue's lap. I'll just pretend I'm playing basketball.*

Zac was an excellent basketball player. But this was a high-pressure shot. Zac kept imagining Caz laughing at him. *You'll never make it*, she was saying in his mind.

But Zac ignored the voice. He had to

make this shot. Sure, being a spy was a drag sometimes. But like it or not Zac Power was a GIB agent and he had a mission to complete. He took a deep breath and lined up the shot. Then he threw the diamond at the statue of the Golden Sun King.

From the moment it left his hands Zac realised he'd made a mistake. He'd thrown it way too hard! Of course, if he had been on the GIB basketball court this wouldn't have mattered. It would have just hit the backboard and bounced in but today there was no backboard for the diamond to bounce off.

There was just the statue's head.

CRRRRRACK!

The diamond hit the statue right in the face. Zac held his breath, waiting to see what would happen next.

As if in slow motion the diamond rolled down the statue and into its hands. It wobbled there for a long moment. Zac could hardly watch. Would it stay put or would it end up rolling into the pit?

Finally, the diamond stopped wobbling. Zac leapt in the air. Awesome shot! He wished there was someone to high-five.

The moment the diamond was safely back in its place the cobras disappeared into the trench and the scorpions ran straight past Zac and back down the holes in the walls.

Zac wanted to sigh with relief. But he couldn't just yet. He had to check that the statue was OK.

From a distance the statue looked perfect. He put 'Snake Charming Song' on and jumped over the pit. Up close Zac could see that there was a huge crack all the way around the statue's neck. When he pushed the head it fell into his hands. *Oh no! I must have broken it with the diamond!*

Another earth tremor forced Zac to jump out of the way of the falling rocks. Zac coughed. His lungs were filling up with dust. He knew he should be finding a way out. But he didn't want to leave before he fixed the statue. It was going to be hard enough to explain to GIB about letting Caz escape. He didn't want to tell them that he'd accidentally wrecked this statue too.

Zac tipped his Pyramid-Pack upside down and shook it.

This was his last hope. Perhaps there was something in it that would be perfect for instantly fixing a broken statue.

The only thing to fall out of the bag was Zac's Super-Strength Hair Gel.

Zac felt his hair. It was still in perfect condition; even after all he'd been through. The hair gel was really strong stuff. *But is it strong enough to fix a 2000-year-old statue?* There was nothing for it but to try.

Zac quickly squeezed the tube of Super-Strength Hair Gel onto the statue's neck. Then he squished the head back on top.

To Zac's relief the gel set instantly. When he checked the head a moment later it was firmly stuck in place.

Zac smiled. There hadn't been a hair crisis yet that this gel couldn't solve!

The SpyPad beeped a warning.

Zac had seven minutes to get out. He turned around, ready to run for the door. But before he had a chance to escape, the pyramid shook again and a huge pile of rocks and sand came crashing down in front of him.

CRRAAAASHHHHH!

When the dust cleared Zac couldn't see
a tunnel any more.

He was trapped!

CHAPTER 10

There was no time for Zac to dig his way out. He was totally stuck! *Unless there's another way out?* thought Zac.

In a flash he remembered something else about *Pyramid Panic*. Whenever he played the game it was always the Treasure Room that he was ejected from.

He frowned, thinking hard. What caused

him to be ejected? The only thing that he could remember was that he always seemed to trip over just before he found himself flying through the air.

The SpyPad had begun a warning countdown. Zac started pacing as quickly as he could around the room, looking for a clue.

Then suddenly he found himself sprawled on the ground.

SMACK!

He'd tripped, just like when he played *Pyramid Panic*!

He looked down and saw two footprints carved into the stone he'd tripped on. The stone looked a bit like a welcome mat. But Zac knew that it was more like an *un*welcome mat.

Zac jumped on the stone and put his feet onto the carved footprints.

Immediately a panel in the ceiling creaked backwards and a light streamed through. It was so bright that at first Zac couldn't see anything.

Where was that light coming from? Then he realised. It was sunlight! This must be a tunnel leading up to the tip of the pyramid!

The stone beneath Zac's feet started pulling back slowly into the ground. Then suddenly it shot forward again, shooting Zac up into the air.

Zac flew into the tunnel above his head. He couldn't stop smiling. This was wicked! He felt like a ball in a pinball machine.

When he opened his eyes again he was out in the sunshine, high above the pyramid.

Zac looked down at the pyramid. Was it going to collapse? That would be *really* annoying after all the effort he'd put into saving the statue.

The seconds ticked past but the pyramid didn't collapse. In fact, it remained as solid as it had for centuries. He'd made it out just in time!

The pyramid was saved!

Then Zac looked down again.

Uh oh! He remembered that what goes

up, must come down. He was now hurtling towards the ground.

He could see his dune buggy far below him, looking like a toy. But it was getting bigger by the second. If he kept falling like this he was going to end up squashed like a bug on the windscreen.

Zac quickly thought back to what he had learned in Spy School about crash landing. He tucked his head down into his knees in the brace position.

Then he heard a strange noise. It was like a bird trying to flap its wings. It was coming from his Pyramid-Pack!

There was the sound of ripping material.

Suddenly Zac wasn't falling any more. He was gliding!

Zac looked over his shoulder and smiled. There had been one last thing in his Pyramid-Pack that he hadn't noticed. A paraglider! The chute had opened up automatically as he started plummeting towards the ground.

Now I can enjoy myself, thought Zac. He did a couple of loop-the-loops and circled the pyramid below him. Then he guided the glider carefully down towards the dune buggy. He pulled up in a perfect 10-point move and dropped right into the driver's seat.

Zac checked the solar power levels. The

battery was completely charged again. He had more than enough energy to get back to base camp and meet up with his family. In fact, there was probably enough power to take the long way home and jump a few more sand dunes!

But there was one last thing he had to do. Zac untied the knot in the beetle-torch and let the scarab beetles out. In a flash they jumped off the buggy and burrowed down into the sand.

As Zac watched them disappear, the SpyPad's satellite phone rang.

'It's Agent Bum Smack here,' said a very familiar voice. 'Where are you, Zac? There's a big pile of dishes here at base camp. And according to the roster it's your turn to wash them.'

Zac sighed. It looked like the sand dunes would have to wait.

'OK, mum,' he said. 'I'm on my way.'

ZAC POWER

LUNAR STRIKE

CHAPTER 1

Zac Power had his SpyPad earphones jammed in tight, and his eyes closed.

Screaming, loud electric guitar music drowned out all other sounds. Zac was in another world – Axe Grinder's world!

He was tilted back dangerously in his classroom chair, his feet up on the desk. It was lunchtime on Friday – the school week was nearly over. Zac was listening to his favourite band's new single for the 86th time that day!

Sonic Boom was Axe Grinder's latest track. It was so new that it had only been released at midnight the previous day. Zac's older brother Leon had downloaded it at four seconds past midnight. Computer stuff was easy for Leon — he was a spy.

In fact, the whole Power family were spies. Zac liked to think of himself as a SUPER spy. An expert in keeping cool at all times. Always on the lookout for danger. Able to escape the trickiest traps and capture any villain.

The Power family worked for GIB, the

Government Investigation Bureau. Leon took care of everything on the technical side. This left Zac to tackle all the toughest missions.

But GIB was the last thing on Zac's mind. He was concentrating on every note of *Sonic Boom*. Everyone knew that Ricky Blaze, Axe Grinder's guitarist, was the hottest player alive. One day Zac hoped he would be that good, too.

After six months of nagging them, Zac's parents had bought him a totally wicked, ruby-red Gibson Firebird electric guitar. But the new guitar came with a catch – Zac had to attend boring old guitar lessons early *every* Saturday morning. Yawn!

'Zac Power!'

Zac opened his eyes in surprise. His teacher, Mrs Tran, was standing in front of his desk, scowling.

'Take your earphones out *now*,' she said.

This was no way to treat a super spy and future guitar hero! Trouble was, Zac could never say a word about GIB or his missions. No-one at school knew about the action-packed life he led, not even his closest friends. Keeping his identity secret was too important for his spy work.

'Sorry, Mrs Tran,' said Zac.

'Never mind that. The school nurse told me that you missed an important vaccination when you took a day off last month,' said Mrs Tran sternly.

She looked as though she was enjoying herself when she added, 'Off you go to sick bay – she's going to give you the injection immediately.'

OUCH!

Zac headed out of the classroom and walked slowly down the hall. All thoughts of Axe Grinder's incredible new song were swept away by the idea of a big, sharp needle.

He wasn't even halfway to sick bay when a hand reached out of the cleaner's cupboard and grabbed his collar. Zac was yanked in among the brooms and buckets.

The door slammed shut behind him.

A small flashlight lit up the tiny cupboard. When Zac recognised the face of GIB Agent Tripwire, he breathed a sigh of relief.

'Sorry about the scare, Zac,' whispered Agent Tripwire. 'We've got an emergency and had to pull you out of class as fast as possible.'

'So no needle, then?' asked Zac. 'And I get to skip the rest of school?'

'No needle, no school, and keep your voice down,' hissed the GIB man.

Agent Tripwire reached across to a dusty shelf. He lifted up a can of Squeezy Shine floor polish. Zac heard a click.

The whole shelf moved away from the cupboard wall to reveal a hidden doorway. Zac could just make out a steep concrete ramp that led to the school car-park.

Agent Tripwire jumped into the darkness. Zac headed down the ramp after him. A few seconds later Zac heard a gigantic motor roar into life. A powerful headlight came on.

The GIB agent was twisting the throttle on an *ABSOLUTELY* **HUGE** motorbike.

'Let's move,' said Agent Tripwire.

He threw Zac a strange-looking helmet and pointed to the seat behind him. In a second they were flying out of the

carpark at top speed. Zac was holding on
for his life!

CHAPTER 2

Agent Tripwire's voice sounded in the speakers built into Zac's high-tech helmet.

'We have to get you to the Air Force base right away,' said Agent Tripwire. 'The Lightning Strike here is the quickest way to cut through traffic.'

Zac had heard rumours of the Lightning Strike ultra-bike — a top-secret, high-speed vehicle being developed at GIB headquarters. The ultra-bike was painted a rich, dark blue. It packed a motor larger than most helicopters did. Sparkling silver exhaust pipes stretched down the sides.

They were moving so fast Zac could barely suck in enough air to breathe. They passed cars in a blur. Agent Tripwire leaned the massive bike on its side as they tore around corners.

'We've been messaging you on your SpyPad since 7 a.m.' Agent Tripwire was annoyed.

GIB agents were required to carry their SpyPad Turbo Deluxe 3000 with them at all times.

While it looked like an ordinary handheld computer game, the SpyPad was an amazing piece of electronic equipment. A satellite phone, super-computer, X-ray machine, laser, voice scrambler and dozens of other things – all in one small unit.

Zac didn't say anything. He guessed he hadn't heard the messages while he was listening to Axe Grinder's music.

'You've lost a lot of valuable time on this mission,' said Agent Tripwire. 'You did have a full 24 hours but now you've got barely 18 hours and 27 minutes left to get the job done.'

Zac looked over Agent Tripwire's shoulder. The GIB agent was working the touch-screen computer between the Lightning Strike's handlebars. The screen showed dozens of complex words and numbers. Zac noticed their speed – 256 kilometres an hour. This was an awesome ride!

'I'm uploading your mission details to the Stealth Master helmet you're wearing,' said Agent Tripwire. 'You'll like the helmet, Zac. Built in mini-computer, speakers, microphone and camera. Read-outs for air supply and pressure. Special infrared, ultra-violet, heat and night vision.'

Zac's helmet visor blinked on, and his mission began to scroll up the screen.

CLASSIFIED

MISSION INITIATED: 7 A.M.

GIB's WorldEye satellite has photographed BIG's secret new base on the Moon. Intelligence suggests that BIG plans to use the base to sabotage the worldwide webcast of the Rockathon, and steal billions of dollars in donations. BIG's mystery agent, Mirror, broke into the SpaceFortress a few hours ago.

YOUR MISSION:

Proceed immediately to the SpaceFortress and stop Agent Mirror. Prevent theft of donations and sabotage of Rockathon.

~ END ~

BIG was the sworn enemy of GIB. It was just like BIG to come up with such a plan. Billions in donations to the Rockathon would be a tasty haul for BIG.

The Rockathon was a massive charity event to raise money for countries struck by a tsunami. This freak tidal wave had left thousands of people homeless and starving.

The Rockathon featured the hottest bands from 28 countries. They would perform at a gigantic open-air concert. A few thousand very lucky people would get to watch the show live. The rest of the world could see it on the internet webcast. Coolest of all, Axe Grinder would be the very first band to play!

Suddenly Zac was almost thrown over the side of the Lightning Strike. Agent Tripwire had slammed on the brakes and the ultra-bike went into a slide. It skidded to a halt less than a metre from the loading ramp of a giant Hercules transport plane.

They were on the runway of the Air Force base. Agent Shadow marched down the ramp. 'A quick question for you, Zac,' said Agent Shadow with a worried look on his face. 'Do you know how long astronauts train for their first trip into space?'

'Hmmm,' said Zac. 'I think about three years, at least.'

'That's a shame,' said Agent Shadow.
'I'm giving you three HOURS!'

CHAPTER 3

Keep cool, Zac thought to himself. He had been on some crazy adventures before, but never **SPACE!**

Now aboard the Hercules, Zac took off his Stealth Master helmet and looked around. This was no ordinary transport plane. The inside of the aircraft was like a cross between an enormous gym and a lab.

Unusual training gear, advanced computer equipment and at least 10 scientists in white coats lined the gleaming walls. You could park three semi-trailers inside the plane and still have room for a ... Leon!

Zac's older brother was sitting in front of a computer screen. He was busily tapping away at a keyboard, as usual.

'What are you doing here?' asked Zac.

'Oh, hi,' said Leon. 'That Lightning Strike is mighty quick, isn't it. My job is to take you through the equipment for this mission. I'll also help with your training. I think you're going to be very surprised.'

'I'm already surprised,' said Zac. 'A few minutes ago I was off to see the nurse.

Now I find out I'll be in space in three hours!'

The surprises kept coming. Zac saw a small, pink nose poke out of Leon's jacket pocket. Whiskers on the nose twitched and then a whole head popped out for a look around. A rat's head!

'Looks like everyone's along for this mission,' said Zac pointing at the rat. 'Even our pet!'

The rat was Cipher, the smallest member of the Power family.

'I had to bring him along,' said Leon, tickling Cipher under the chin. 'I could tell he was feeling lonely and there was no-one home to ratty-sit him.'

Cipher scampered onto a desk and started munching on a Chocmallow Puff. It was the size of his head! Chocmallow Puffs were Zac's favourite breakfast cereal. It looked like they were Cipher's as well.

'Family reunion is over, boys,' said Agent Shadow impatiently. 'Here's the deal: we know that BIG has a new secret base on the Moon called Lunar Strike. BIG will use the Lunar Strike base to somehow cause chaos on the internet.'

'Sounds like a distraction to me,' said Zac.

'Exactly,' said Agent Shadow. 'What they're really after is money from the

Rockathon. BIG's Agent Mirror is already inside the Space Fortress, organising the robbery.'

Leon continued. 'The Space Fortress is a heavily guarded bank computer that orbits Earth. Seconds after the Rockathon begins, millions of dollars in donations will be sent, via the internet, from all parts of the world. All the donations will pass through the Space Fortress. That's where BIG will steal the money from!'

'We don't have exact details,' added Agent Shadow. 'That's what makes this mission so dangerous. We know next to nothing about this Agent Mirror. Obviously there's not enough time for you to get to the Moon, so your only chance is to get into the Space Fortress.'

Leon looked worried. 'All security is computer-controlled on the Space Fortress. Motion detectors, laser canons, tracking missiles, space torpedos – the works! The whole space station is encased in armour plating one metre thick. We don't know how Agent Mirror got in, but he's already tampered with the master controls!'

'Time is tight, Zac,' added Agent Shadow. 'Three hours training is all we can afford to give you. The Rockathon begins at 7 p.m. tomorrow night – on the other side of the world. With the 12-hour time difference, you MUST complete the mission by 7 a.m. tomorrow – no later!'

'Oh,' said Leon, 'and Mum – I mean Agent Bum Smack – says you have to be home by 8 a.m. to get to guitar practice!'

Zac rolled his eyes. 'Great!'

CHAPTER 4

'Leon will brief you on your equipment while we prepare for take-off,' said Agent Shadow briskly. 'You'll be weightless in space and you need to learn to handle it. We'll be airborne in 25 minutes – get cracking.'

'I've got some fantastic gear for you,' said Leon, leading Zac over to a work bench. Four GIB scientists were waiting to help with the demonstration. 'First up, the Space Master. I tweaked the technology of the Chameleon suit that you used on your last mission. I combined it with a space suit of my own design.'

One of the scientists passed over a folded black garment. Leon took it and shook it out.

'I've set it for plain black colouring at the moment,' explained Leon. 'That'll be the best camouflage for moving around undetected in space. The suit is fully pressurised and heated. Space has no air pressure and is dreadfully cold. Without the suit on you'll explode and then freeze into a lot of VERY messy ice-cubes.'

'Nice work, Leon,' said Zac, slipping into the Space Master. 'Light, comfortable, a good fit. It looks sweet in jet black!'

Leon smiled – he was very proud of himself. 'This belt completes the suit,' he added, as another scientist handed over more equipment. 'The buckle controls suit colour, temperature and pressure – quite simple. There's a specially designed pouch for your SpyPad, along with everything else you'll need.'

Zac wrapped the wide belt around his waist and secured the control buckle. He fitted his SpyPad into its pouch. He flipped the top on one of the other pouches and pulled out a tiny, silver cylinder the size of a small battery.

'Ah,' said Leon, going into full nerd mode. 'Your oxygen supply. I've packed you six of those mini-tanks. They're exactly like the air tanks used for underwater diving.'

'They don't look like they hold much air,' said Zac, lifting the cylinder to his ear and shaking it.

'Careful, Zac!' said Leon. 'The oxygen inside is under extreme pressure. That's how we can keep them so small. That mini-tank fits into your Stealth Master helmet and will give you hours of air. Be warned though, you MUST keep them away from excessive heat at all times.'

'Otherwise?' asked Zac, replacing the delicate, teeny tank in its belt pouch.

'That thing could go off like a grenade!' said Leon, looking very serious.

'What about these?' asked Zac, fiddling with a number of small, metal SpyPad discs he had found in another belt pouch.

'My own invention,' smiled Leon. 'They're a selection of nasty computer viruses that you can spread using your SpyPad. Each one comes with its own instructions. I thought they might come in handy.'

The engines of the Hercules began to rumble. Zac and Leon grabbed the workbench to steady themselves as the monstrous plane taxied down the runway.

Agent Shadow returned from the cockpit. 'Everyone strap themselves in good and tight,' he yelled above the engine noise. 'Everyone except you, Zac. Time for your zero gravity training.'

The Hercules climbed steeply and levelled out at high altitude. Agent Shadow gave a nod to one of the scientists, who then hit a switch. Leon and the crew checked their safety belts. The lights inside the Hercules blinked on and off for a split second.

Zac heard a quiet hum in the walls...

and bumped his head on the roof! He hadn't even noticed the zero gravity generators kick in – he was floating six metres above the metal floor!

'This plane is used for astronaut training,' Agent Shadow explained. 'Best place for you to learn.'

Zac hit his bum a few times over the next five minutes. Luckily all those hours Zac had spent surfing meant that he very quickly got used to being upside-down and off balance.

When he got the hang of zero gravity he began zooming about inside the plane. He even swooped Leon and gave him a good fright.

It was like the best fun-park ride ever —
without having to buy a ticket!

Zac was disappointed when he had to
stop. The three-hour session just flew past.

'Time's up,' said Agent Shadow. 'There's
barely 14 hours to complete this mission.
Let's introduce you to your last piece of
equipment.'

CHAPTER 5

'Bring it up,' said Agent Shadow, signalling one of GIB scientists. A metal trapdoor in the belly of the plane slid to one side. A hydraulic platform rose through the floor.

Before Zac was an extraordinary, futuristic spacecraft, painted blazing yellow and red.

'All right!' he said, excited.

Agent Shadow led Zac over to the spacecraft. 'This is the Star Master, GIB's mini-space shuttle. It's the smallest vehicle capable of manned space flight. You'll be taking it out for the first test run, Agent Rock Star.'

Zac leapt into the cockpit of the Star Master. 'I can't wait to get this beauty up to top speed,' said Zac, running one hand down the smooth hull of the spacecraft.

It had the lean looks of a jet fighter and the rocket engine muscle of an advanced NASA shuttle.

Zac immediately began punching some buttons and running pre-flight safety checks. He booted up the navigation computer, checked the star maps and programmed a course to the Space Fortress. After fitting his Stealth Master helmet, he gave the thumbs up.

'Drop the ramp and I'll power up the rockets,' said Zac, keen to get moving. 'Anything else I need to know?'

'Be very careful approaching the Space Fortress,' warned Agent Shadow. 'The station's sensors will detect anything — human or machine — that comes near. If you're not careful, you'll be blasted to space dust!'

'Here,' said Leon, passing over the cereal box. 'Take the Chocmallow Puffs in case you need a snack. Good luck!'

Zac sealed the cockpit of the Star Master. Everyone stood well back. The loading ramp on the Hercules opened slowly and a strong wind rushed inside the plane. Zac pressed the ignition buttons and the rockets thundered.

Zac gripped the joystick and edged the Star Master forward. He hit the mini-shuttle's throttle on the final few metres of the ramp. The spacecraft dropped out into the sky and fired upwards.

The speed was incredible. Soon the Hercules was a speck in the distance. It wouldn't be too long before he reached the outer atmosphere. Zac made himself comfortable and bent down for the box of Chocmallow Puffs. He hadn't eaten anything since lunchtime. The zero gravity training was a tough workout and his stomach was grumbling.

Something inside the cereal box wriggled. Zac let go of the joystick in fright. The Star Master swivelled onto its back and dived towards the ground!

Zac planted his feet firmly on the floor. He yanked on the joystick and wrestled the mini-shuttle back under control. Chocmallow Puffs flew about the cockpit and the box landed on his knees. A furry bundle jumped out into his lap.

'Cipher!' said Zac in surprise.

At some point during the zero gravity training session the rat must have crawled inside the cereal box, looking for food. Now Zac had an extra passenger.

'This is a dangerous mission!' Zac scolded the rat. 'I can't have stowaways along for the ride.'

Cipher's nose wiggled, his little black eyes blinked.

Zac checked the time. It was 7.09 p.m. He had less than 12 hours to get the job done. He couldn't turn back just to drop off his pet rat!

The sky began to darken. The mini-shuttle was moments from entering space.

'All right, Cipher,' said Zac. 'I hope you

can follow orders. You're about to become the world's first rat-stronaut.'

CHAPTER 6

The Star Master was surrounded by darkness. Zac gazed at the stars. They were astoundingly bright with no air pollution in the way. He banked the mini-shuttle to get one last look at Earth. It was a colossal, glowing ball in blue, green and white. Maybe he could do some space sightseeing on the trip back.

Within a few hours Zac was getting near the Space Fortress.

I really don't feel like dodging laser canons and space torpedoes, Zac thought. *I need to find somewhere close by to leave the shuttle, then I can space-hop over to the Space Fortress in secret.*

Zac checked the computer's star maps for a good place to park. His best bet was an asteroid field nearby.

In another 25 minutes they had reached the asteroid field. The Star Master coasted right into the middle of the swarm of swiftly moving rocks.

'Hey, Cipher,' said Zac, jerking the joystick left and right to avoid colliding with the rocks. 'This is just like my *Pluto Pilot* computer game – but a whole lot better!'

Asteroids came at the mini-shuttle from all directions. There were hundreds of them. Some were the size of a basketball, others were bigger than a house! Zac kept the Star Master ducking and diving through the field of space rocks.

He located an asteroid that looked like it could hide a bulldozer. An excellent parking spot. Zac pulled the mini-shuttle alongside and gently touched down.

Zac looked at the time. It was 11.41 p.m.

Zac carefully scooped up the rat. He pulled out the collar of his Space Master suit and tucked Cipher down the front. Zac loaded his helmet with one of the tiny oxygen tanks and hit the emergency release on the cockpit canopy. He unfastened his seat belt and felt himself drift upwards.

Zac crab-walked across the asteroid. On the other side of the jumbo space rock he made a very interesting discovery. Clamped firmly to the rough surface of the asteroid was a spacecraft. It was painted a girly pink, with flowers all over it. 'Double Trouble' was sprayed along the side.

'Hey, Cipher,' said Zac with a laugh. 'This Agent Mirror tough guy is flying a Barbie rocket!'

Zac moved closer to check out the spacecraft. It was a decent ship, looked fast and had a roomy cockpit. But it was no Star Master.

Zac hid behind a rocky ledge. He peeked carefully over the top into the endless space beyond. In the distance, there it was – the Space Fortress.

It *was* a fortress! Zac could make out the laser canons sweeping back and forth, looking for a target. Dozens of tracking missiles poked from lethal launchers. It bristled with satellite antennae, radar dishes and aerials.

The sensors must be set to pick up human intruders and spacecraft only! thought Zac.

Zac realised the sensors would have to ignore the asteroids, otherwise the automatic security computer would waste all day zapping every speck of space dust that came within range.

All I have to do is hitch a ride on a rock, thought Zac.

Zac tapped the controls of his SpyPad and began scanning some nearby asteroids. He needed something the size of a small car – big enough to stay hidden behind until the last minute. He locked in the perfect asteroid.

Zac sprung from his hiding place. He somersaulted twice and landed like a ninja on his chosen rock.

CHAPTER 7

Cipher did NOT enjoy being in space. He fidgeted about inside Zac's suit, squirmed under his arm and down the sleeve.

'Hey, hold still,' said Zac, gripping the asteroid. 'That tickles!'

The speeding asteroid was drawing close to the Space Fortress. Any second now Zac would have to ditch his ride and leap onto the hull of the huge space station. He relaxed his grip on the rock and curled into a ball. He hoped his rolling motion would fool the security sensors long enough to land on the Space Fortress.

Zac landed with a soft thud. He was out of immediate danger. The security system wouldn't shoot a tracking missile at itself! Scuttling quietly across the Space Fortress, he spotted a maintenance hatch.

Zac flicked the SpyPad selector to Laser and used it as a cutting torch. The Space Fortress was protected by solid steel, but the small hatch was attached to a couple of hinges that melted like cheap chocolate.

The red-hot metal cooled quickly in

the bitter cold of space. Zac tugged the hatch back and slipped inside. He found himself in a tight tunnel used for electrical cables. Taking care not to squish Cipher, Zac crawled forwards until he discovered an airlock into the Space Fortress.

Inside the airlock, Zac took off his Stealth Master helmet. He felt around inside his space suit and grabbed Cipher. Out in the light the rat let out a tiny sneeze and blinked in confusion. Zac dropped him into the helmet for safety.

The Space Fortress was like an immense maze. Passageways lead in every direction. He needed to stay camouflaged. He spun the buckle-dial on his Space Master suit and changed the colour to match the white walls.

Zac came across countless rooms full of complex equipment. He lost valuable time searching for clues to BIG's plan — and Agent Mirror.

Zac moved silently down a long white corridor, looking for the control centre. A murmur at the far end of the corridor caught his attention. Activating the multi-directional microphone on his SpyPad, Zac tuned in to the conversation. He could make out a voice coming through from the distant Lunar Strike base on the Moon.

'We have the Electromagnetic Pulse Beam on standby,' said the voice, crackling across space. 'We will activate on your signal. I need a situation report, Agent Mirror.'

Zac crept closer to the room where the conversation came from, and took a gamble. He poked his SpyPad around the corner of the open door and snapped a quick photo with the built-in camera.

Crouching in the corridor he checked the photo on the screen. What he saw amazed him.

On the SpyPad screen were two girls – identical twin girls!

'Pinky only needs a little more preparation before she can commence hacking into the Space Fortress system,' said one of the girls.

'Superb work,' replied the voice from Lunar Strike. 'Britney, once we scramble the webcast you will have less than five minutes to steal the Rockathon donations. We need that money swiftly transferred from the Space Fortress account to our secret BIG account. Gone without a trace. Understood?'

'You can count on it,' promised Britney.

Zac had never expected this. The mysterious BIG agent was actually a pair of girls? Now was a good time to check in with GIB headquarters. Zac sneaked back the way he'd come.

He ducked into an empty storage locker and dialled Leon's direct number using the

SpyPad's satellite phone.

'Zac, any news?' asked his brother, as soon as he appeared on the screen.

'Big news,' whispered Zac. 'And I mean BIG news. Agent Mirror is actually twin girls, called Pinky and Britney! I don't have much time. I overheard some of their plan. What can you tell me about an Electromagnetic Pulse Beam?'

'EPB, eh? Interesting,' said Leon. 'Latest weapons technology. If they have one, the Lunar Strike base could send out a concentrated electromagnetic burst aimed at Earth. Harmless to humans but totally fries all electronic equipment. A single EPB blast would crash every computer running the Rockathon webcast.'

'Thanks for the tip. I'm going to – '

But Zac never finished the sentence. Two metal claws closed around him, pinning his arms to his side. He struggled to break free.

The more he struggled, the tighter the claws gripped him. Zac could see stars – but they weren't in space!

CHAPTER

Zac's feet thrashed about in mid-air. He looked around at his captor, and saw that it was a **_HUGE ROBOT._**

The robot towered above him, as tall as a professional basketballer. It was built like a tank but was also painted dazzling pink – the same colour as the Double Trouble rocket.

The robot had arms that belonged on a construction crane. They ended in lethal claws that could obviously crush a car.

The robot was carrying him straight back down to the room he'd been spying on. Struggling to remain upright, he saw the twin girls step into the corridor.

'Intruder located and captured!' said an artificial voice behind his head.

'Drop him!' commanded the one called Britney.

Zac hit the cold floor, face first. It was wonderful to be able to move his arms again.

'Zac Power, I presume?' said the other one, Pinky.

'So this is the spy Lunar Strike warned us might show up,' said Britney, narrowing her beady eyes. 'You don't look like much. Certainly nothing Boltz here can't handle.'

Zac wobbled to his feet and massaged his arms, remembering the claws closing around them.

'So, BIG is still hiring girls?' said Zac, thinking of Caz, the last BIG agent he had encountered.

'Oh, BIG is hiring A LOT of girls,' giggled Britney, winking at her sister. 'Rockets, robots and robbery – that's our business. Right, sis?' She turned to Pinky for a high five.

'At the moment it's robbery,' continued Britney. 'But what say we take a break? We have some time to kill before we can transfer the money. Boltz, bring our guest into the control room. Be gentle – no need for the Gorilla Grip this time.'

Boltz lifted Zac and tucked him under one arm, like you would a bag of chips. It clunked into the control room and tossed Zac into a chair.

'The money transfer will go through in a few hours,' said Pinky. 'Then we'll leave you in peace. Of course, you will be trapped on this space station. But if you behave yourself, we'll play nice and leave you with enough oxygen to breathe.'

'We'll let GIB know where you are,' continued Britney. 'Although when we're finished with you, it might be a bit embarrassing facing a rescue crew. Because, Zac, it's time for – '

'EXTREME MAKE-OVER!' squealed the sisters, clapping their hands.

Pinky fetched a large bag of cosmetics. Britney gave Boltz a nod. The mechanical monstrosity moved in behind the chair and pinned Zac's arms behind him.

'You won't be needing this with what we've got in mind,' said Pinky, snatching Zac's helmet and chucking it into a corner.

She began teasing up Zac's hair with a comb as she whistled an annoying Taylor

Swift tune. Britney got to work with mascara and eye-shadow.

Zac watched precious time tick away on the control room clock. It was already 3.33 p.m. He couldn't believe he was in space, having a make-over at the hands of BIG twin girls!

Pinky was busy spraying Zac's hair with hairspray and using a pencil to colour in his eyebrows.

This is getting ridiculous, Zac thought.

Britney was colouring his cheeks rosy red. On went the dabs of lipstick.

Make these crazy twins stop! thought Zac, wondering how long they could keep this up.

'One more touch,' cackled Pinky, adding so much black pencil around Zac's eyes that he looked like a frightened panda when the girls triumphantly held up a mirror to show Zac.

'C'mon, sis,' said Britney. 'We better head down to the central computer and get ready to scoop the loot!'

Zac looked at the clock again. There were only two and a bit hours left to save the Rockathon. *Will that be enough time?*

The Mirror twins skipped out of the control room, leaving Boltz to watch over Zac.

Zac could hear the metal beast's brain whirring –

Then he heard another sound. He looked down to see Cipher darting between the robot's feet. Boltz saw the rat at the same instant.

No! thought Zac. *I'll be scraping poor Cipher off the floor.*

But Boltz let out a scream that echoed around the control room. Cipher had chewed through the robot's balance cable. It wobbled and then tipped over, crashing to the floor. Flames started shooting from its ears!

CHAPTER

'Cipher, my hero!' whooped Zac, leaping to his feet.

But the rat took one look at Zac and scampered back to the safety of the Stealth Master helmet.

'Do I really look that bad?' asked Zac, touching his frizzy hair.

He reached into his backpack and found a tissue, then used it to wipe off the worst of the make-up. He ran a hand through his hair to smooth it down as best he could.

Boltz was out cold, but Zac wasn't taking any chances. He knelt down beside the fallen robot and whipped out his SpyPad. Using the laser he cut through the hatch at the top of its head and unplugged its electronic brain. A final wisp of smoke curled up from the trashed machine and it sagged in a sad heap.

Crunch time. Zac needed to work fast. He dug out the handful of Leon's virus discs and slotted one into his SpyPad. The screen came to life.

CLASSIFIED
– GIB COMPUTER VIRUS –

*Hello, and welcome to the **Mindwarp Worm**. The **Worm** seeks out the source of any unauthorised access and attacks the hacker's own equipment.*

Guaranteed to cause the total collapse of all known computer programs, wipe all hard drives and destroy all files.

Have a nice day, and thank you for choosing this quality Leon Power virus!

~ END ~

'Sounds nasty,' said Zac, looking over at Cipher. 'If the *Mindwarp Worm* does what it says, we could ruin the Rockathon robbery AND fry all the computers on the Lunar Strike base.'

Zac moved over to the control console and plugged in his SpyPad. He set it to Voice Scrambler. He would still have a sample of Britney talking, from eavesdropping on their conversation. If he could fool the BIG people at Lunar Strike for a few seconds, his plan would work.

Zac cleared his throat and spoke into the SpyPad. 'Testing, testing.'

He surprised himself. The voice that came from the SpyPad speakers was high and whiny – but sounded more like Pinky. It'd do nicely.

He contacted the base. 'Lunar Strike, this is Space Fortress, please respond.'

'This is Lunar Strike. Go ahead, Space Fortress.'

'BIG hacking preparation is complete,' fibbed Zac. 'Request that you network with our central computer for final check.'

'Roger that,' came the reply. 'Network link operational. Lunar Strike out.'

Zac was cutting it close!

He used his SpyPad to inspect the computer files. He discovered that Pinky had already hacked into the system on the Space Fortress and was connected to BIG's secret account. She was all set to steal the Rockathon donations, as easily as taking money out of an ATM.

And that was her mistake!

Zac clicked on the secret BIG account and reversed the transfer. Instead of money going OUT of the Rockathon account, suddenly billions of dollars were being donated to the victims of the tsunami – by a very generous organisation called BIG!

Zac gave a satisfied laugh as he loaded up the *Mindwarp Worm*. He hit send, and Leon's devilish virus went to work.

Within seconds, a panicked voice from Lunar Strike came through the speakers. 'Space Fortress, we have a problem!

Please respond urgently! We are getting severe malfunctions all across the base! Space Fortress, can you provide any information?!'

'This is Space Fortress,' said Zac into the microphone. 'I have some information for you. Eat *Worm*, hackers!'

Suddenly, Zac heard very annoyed shrieks coming down the corridor. The *Mindwarp Worm* had obviously gone to work on Pinky and Britney's equipment as well. They would probably have spotted Zac's 'withdrawal' from BIG's account, too.

Time to bug out, thought Zac, quickly grabbing his helmet and Cipher, and running out of the room.

CHAPTER 10

'Boltz! My beautiful baby Boltz!' wailed Pinky.

Zac glanced back over his shoulder as he raced down the corridor. The Mirror twins were standing in the doorway of the control room staring at the wrecked robot.

'Power, you're finished!' screamed Britney.

Zac broke into a sprint. He dropped Cipher down the front of his Space Master suit as he ran. 'Sorry, little pal,' he said to the rat. 'It's the last time you'll have to travel in my armpit, I promise.'

With his SpyPad set to Locator, Zac scanned the Space Fortress, looking for a likely escape airlock.

'Down here for 20 metres, up two levels, turn right, then straight ahead!'

In a minute, Zac had his helmet back on and was out in space. He looked around for a passing asteroid that would take him back to his mini-shuttle. With some frantic space dog-paddling, and even some galactic back-stroke, he made it!

Zac knew the furious Mirror twins weren't far behind. He jumped into the Star Master and sealed the cockpit. He punched the engine ignition button. He did a sweeping turn around the Space Fortress and pointed the mini-shuttle towards Earth.

The Double Trouble rocket was right on the tail of the Star Master for a few moments until –

KABOOOOOOOOM!

Zac breathed a sigh of relief as he looked in the rear-vision mirror. The twins had crashed the Double Trouble into an asteroid and damaged the engine – a smoking tangle of metal was where the tail fin used to be! In the rocket's cockpit he could just make out Pinky and Britney, red-faced and bellowing, making *very* rude gestures in his direction.

Zac lifted Cipher out of his suit. 'Couldn't have done it without my robo-buster rat!' he said, putting Cipher on the floor.

His SpyPad beeped. 'Zac, Agent Bum Smack here,' said his mum. 'I hope you remember you have a guitar lesson this morning!'

'Sure, Mum,' groaned Zac, trying to sound interested. 'I'm on my way now.'

He hung up the phone.

Zac couldn't believe he was in *space*,

and had just escaped from those maniac Mirror twins, and was still stuck with a boring guitar lesson!

Suddenly Zac had a thought. As he steered the Star Master through the Earth's upper atmosphere, he made a decision. He set a course for the other side of the world ... and the Rockathon!

If he was quick he could catch the end of Axe Grinder's set and still make it to his guitar lesson. Even if he missed his lesson, surely watching Ricky Blazes live in concert would be the greatest guitar lesson he could ever have?

There was a short landing strip right near the massive outdoor stadium. Zac could see the private jets and helicopters of all the stars lined up beside the runway. He touched down and taxied skilfully to the far end.

Zac bolted towards the stadium. He set his Space Master suit colour back to black. It wasn't much of a disguise but it would have to do.

It was sell-out show. Zac wondered how he'd get inside the stadium without a ticket. He was sneaking around the backstage area when he was stopped by a muscle-bound security guard.

'This way, this way! Quickly, Mr Blazes!' said the bouncer, taking Zac by the arm.

Zac was very confused, but didn't argue.

'Here he is!' the guard called out to a worried-looking stage manager.

Now Zac was utterly bewildered.

'Really, Ricky,' said the stage manager, obviously quite annoyed. 'We told you not to move too far from the stage. The rest of the band is waiting to go back on stage to play the encore.' The stage manager passed Zac a guitar, and helped him strap it on.

'There's been a mistake,' Zac tried to explain. 'I'm not who you think – '

But the stage manager wouldn't listen. He pushed Zac up a short flight of stairs that led to the stage. 'Just one encore, *Sonic Boom*,' he whispered. 'The boys are counting on you to do an extra special job. Hey, where did you get that rat? Nice touch! The crowd will go berserk.'

The whole bizarre situation was becoming clear to Zac. Black jumpsuit, cool hair, outrageous eyeliner. He and Ricky Blazes looked like twin brothers!

Suddenly Zac caught a glimpse of the real Ricky Blazes sitting in a dim corner. He was gulping down a cold drink and paying no attention to the madness going on around him.

Before Zac could utter another word the stage manager pushed him on stage. The roar of thousands of people shook the stage as Zac took his place next to the band's singer.

Axe Grinder's lead singer yelled into the microphone. 'This is the first ever live performance of our new single. I hope you're ready to ROCK!'

Listening to *Sonic Boom* 86 times in a row had finally paid off. Zac knew every note by heart. He leapt about the stage, making sure that the billions of people watching the webcast would never forget THIS Axe Grinder show!

When Cipher climbed onto Zac's shoulder, and then hopped onto his head, the huge crowd erupted like a volcano! Hundreds of stage divers and crowd surfers flew in every direction and the applause was deafening.

By the time he was finished, Zac was dripping with sweat and shaking with excitement.

The song seemed to fly by. Next thing Zac knew he was being helped off stage by the road crew. All the members of Axe Grinder were slapping him on the back and congratulating him on his playing. Cipher was still on top of Zac's head.

As they walked back to the change room tent they spotted the real Ricky Blazes wrestling with five security guards.

'Let go of me!' he yelled. 'I told you, I'M RICKY BLAZES!'

'No fans allowed backstage,' said one of the bouncers as they dragged him away.

'Time to go!'

'Fellas, it's been fun,' said Zac, shaking hands with the members of Axe Grinder. He passed the guitar back to the stage manager and pointed towards Ricky Blazes. 'But you should really go and rescue your guitarist.'

The leader singer's jaw dropped.

'Yeah,' said Zac Power with a shrug. 'You see, Cipher and I have a guitar lesson to get to.'

ZAC POWER

HORROR HOUSE

CHAPTER 1

Zac Power rolled his eyes. His brother Leon was standing in the middle of the GIB hardware store, admiring a pair of standard-issue pliers.

'Look at these beauties!' exclaimed Leon.

Sometimes, Zac found it hard to believe that Leon was his brother. It was even harder to believe that Leon was a spy, working for a top-secret spy organisation called the Government Investigation Bureau, or GIB for short.

In fact, everyone in Zac's family was a spy – including Zac himself. He'd been around spies all his life. And he'd never seen one get excited about pliers before.

Still, Leon is more of a GIB inventor than a spy, Zac reminded himself. Leon was an expert in designing new spy gadgets. To him, a hardware store was better than a lolly shop. Especially an exclusive GIB hardware store like this one.

'OK, let's check out the energy-saving light bulbs,' said Leon, reluctantly putting the pliers down. 'Did you know that we can reduce our total annual carbon emissions by a huge amount once we've changed over all the light bulbs in our —'

'Yes, I know,' Zac interrupted. 'You've told me about a thousand times today, Leon.'

Zac glanced down at his watch.

2.13 P.M.

Normally, Zac would have refused to spend his Saturday afternoon with Leon in a hardware store. But today he didn't have much choice. Tomorrow afternoon, Zac's school friends were going to see a movie called *Ghost Fighters*. Zac really wanted to go. He almost never did normal stuff with his friends because he was always going on GIB missions. But his parents had said that he could only go if he helped Leon with his latest geeky project – swapping all the light bulbs in their house for special energy-saving ones.

Trust Leon to be so boring, Zac groaned to himself. He pulled out his SpyPad, the hand-held super tablet that all GIB spies used. Wasn't there an important mission or something that GIB could send him on?

When Zac went to check his messages, though, there was no signal. He gave his SpyPad a shake, but nothing happened.

Zac frowned at the screen. 'I don't think my SpyPad's connected to Headquarters.'

'Maybe your battery is flat,' suggested Leon, studying a very large screwdriver. 'That sometimes kills the signal. There's a recharge station in the store. One of the auto-drive electric buggies will take you straight there.'

Zac shrugged. He didn't think the battery was flat as he'd only charged it yesterday. But it was a good excuse to get away from Leon and his energy-saving light bulbs!

'Back soon, Leon!' he said, throwing his backpack into the front seat of a nearby GIB buggy. He hopped in and selected **Recharge Station** on the destination panel as the buggy zoomed off.

'Recharge Station selected,' an electronic voice said. It looked like the buggy was set to Chat mode. 'Due to unknown causes, the whole city is experiencing power surges. Please note that your SpyPad might be affected.'

ZZZZZT!

Suddenly, there was a loud buzzing noise and the entire store was plunged into total darkness. Even worse, the buggy had gone out of control!

BRRRM!

It raced around the pitch-black hardware store, screeching around corners and bouncing off shelves. Zac wrestled with the controls, trying to find the manual steering wheel. He had no idea why a black-out would make the buggy go crazy. And he had to figure out how to get it to stop!

SCREEEK!

The buggy screeched wildly and pushed through what felt like heavy plastic doors.

There's got to be a handbrake somewhere on this thing, Zac thought. He felt beneath the seat with his hand.

When he found the brake, he gripped it hard and wrenched it upwards. The buggy immediately braked, but instead of stopping, it started spinning wildly.

Oh no, Zac groaned to himself, trying not to fall out of his seat. *Stopping with a handbrake always causes burn-outs!*

He held onto his seat as hard as he could, but he could feel his fingers slipping. He tensed up, preparing to go flying out of the spinning buggy.

Just as he was about to lose his grip completely, the store lights crackled back to life. The buggy did one last doughnut on the concrete floor and then pulled smoothly to a stop. Zac could smell burning rubber in the air.

He carefully climbed out of the buggy and looked around. It seemed that he was in a storage area out the back of the hardware store.

I wonder if my SpyPad's working yet? Zac thought.

He reached into his pocket and took it out. The SpyPad screen flickered to life. He still didn't have a signal. But there was something very strange on the screen. Very strange indeed.

Zac had received a mission on his SpyPad. But it wasn't from GIB!

CHAPTER 2

Zac knew that GIB usually sent out their missions on special coded disks. It was very risky to send a mission directly to a SpyPad because it might be hacked.

But Zac also knew that other spy agencies weren't so careful.

He quickly scanned the message on his SpyPad.

CLASSIFIED

MISSION INITIATED 10 A.M.
CURRENT TIME 2.30 P.M.

BIG data indicates that there is an unusually high level of storm activity at the mansion at 13 Grande Street. Your mission is to investigate the gathering storm clouds.
We suspect that GIB has come up with a gadget to control the weather! The BIG radar predicts that a major storm will break at 10 a.m. tomorrow. You MUST be at the top of the manion when the storm hits to witness what happens.
Go to the mansion immediately to monitor any suspicious activity.
N.B. The mansion is said to be haunted.

~ END ~

Zac's mouth dropped open. *This message was meant for a BIG agent!* But how did it get on his SpyPad? And why did BIG think that GIB were controlling the weather? It didn't seem like a very GIB thing to do.

I guess the power surges must have made my SpyPad pick up a transmission, he thought.

But his SpyPad still didn't have a signal, and Zac's spy senses were tingling. Something wasn't right.

He decided to go straight to 13 Grande Street and check it out. When his SpyPad had a stronger signal, he would call HQ for back-up.

Zac wondered briefly if he should tell Leon where he was going.

No, he thought, rolling his eyes. *Leon is happy looking at light bulbs. I'll call him later.*

First of all, Zac had to figure out how to get to 13 Grande Street.

I suppose I could take that crazy GIB hardware store buggy, but . . .

Then he had a brainwave. He could take a GIB Commuter-Scooter! These were small, zippy scooters that GIB parked at various handy points around the city. They were for emergency spy travel.

Zac looked around. There was bound to be a Commuter-Scooter near the GIB hardware store.

Sure enough, parked across the street was a shiny green scooter with the word *Dragonfly* painted on the side. It wasn't exactly the sort of super-fast, high-tech vehicle that Zac was used to driving. But it would do.

Zac hopped on and swiped the scooter's controls with his GIB ID card.

BROOOOMMMM!

Not bad! Zac grinned. The machine actually had some grunt! He flicked the scooter into gear and took off.

He sped down the city streets. He was pretty sure he knew the way to Grande Street, but he decided to enter the co-ordinates into the GPS anyway.

After a bit of expert driving, Zac noticed that the Dragonfly's left handlebar was suddenly glowing bright green.

I guess that means I should turn left, Zac thought, pressing hard on the accelerator.

The Dragonfly skimmed the road lightly and barely tilted as Zac took the corner at full speed.

The scooter kept telling him when to turn left and right, and pretty soon Zac arrived at the mansion.

Zac parked the Dragonfly on the kerb, looking around as he climbed off. The other houses in the street looked perfectly normal. But the house at 13 Grande Street was *totally* different.

For one thing, it was a huge mansion. It also looked really old and dirty. Zac couldn't imagine anyone ever living there.

'Creepy, isn't it?' said a voice behind him.

Zac jumped. But it was just a sweet old lady, smiling at him. She reminded Zac of his granny, especially because she smelt so strongly of lavender. The only thing slightly weird about her was that she had lots of purple hair. It looked like a wig!

Thinking quickly, Zac pretended to look upset. 'My football went over the fence,' he said. 'I have to get it.'

'You can't go in there, sonny!' exclaimed the old lady, looking horrified. 'It's haunted! Stay well away.'

Then she patted him on the arm and hurried off.

Zac waited until she was out of sight. Then he slipped through the front gate, smirking. Haunted – as if!

That was where this old lady and his granny were different. Zac's granny was a top GIB spy. She would never believe some stupid haunted-house story.

The same went for Zac. And the more he was told to stay out of somewhere, the more determined he was to go in.

I just don't know why BIG want their agent to wait around at this mansion until tomorrow morning, Zac thought, shaking his head. *What am I supposed to do until then?*

CHAPTER 3

Even Zac had to admit that the yard of 13 Grande Street was pretty creepy. Everything was completely still.

Zac touched one of the plants and realised why. It was completely hard — almost like it was made out of stone. And if that wasn't creepy enough, the yard also had a cemetery in it.

The house itself wasn't any nicer. The paint was peeling and the eaves were covered with cobwebs. Right at the top of the house was a tower with a spooky-looking window.

That must be the room that BIG meant, realised Zac, glancing down at his watch.

4.47 P.M.

It was only late afternoon, but already the garden seemed very dark. Thick storm clouds were blocking out the sun. And they seemed particularly thick around the tower at the top of the mansion.

There was a sudden crash of lightning, and rain started drizzling down. Zac raced for the porch.

As he ran, Zac saw two things that would've been enough to make any normal kid turn and run straight home. First, all the lights in the house flashed on. And then, Zac saw the outline of a figure standing at the top window!

Then the lights flickered off and the figure disappeared.

Zac reached the steps leading up to the porch. His heart was pounding. *Not because I'm scared, though*, he told himself. *It's just because I had to run*. He took a deep breath and started walking quietly up the stairs towards the front door.

Lucky I wore my new sound-absorbing Sneaky Sneakers today, he thought.

He knew he had to be extra careful on this mission. His SpyPad still didn't have any signal to HQ, and GIB had no idea where he was.

It was really important that BIG didn't know he was here, either. He was crashing a top-secret BIG mission!

So I guess I'm hiding here for the next 17 hours, Zac thought to himself.

He put his head against the front door and listened. He thought he could hear something moving inside. It was a sort of rustling sound. Was it the figure he'd seen in the tower? Or was it a BIG agent who had received the same mission Zac's SpyPad had?

Suddenly, something hairy brushed against Zac's neck. He spun around. There was an enormous spider web! And right in the middle of the web was a massive spider with two nasty-looking fangs.

Zac shrugged. It was just a huntsman spider, and he wasn't scared of them. Sure, it was huge, but Zac knew it wouldn't bite him.

'Sorry, little fella,' grinned Zac, stepping around the web.

Then Zac remembered something about huntsman spiders that he'd seen on Leon's favourite TV show, *Creepy Creatures*.

Huntsman spiders never spin webs.
They catch their prey by chasing them.

This spider has a web, thought Zac, *so it must be a fake!* He reached carefully into the web and grabbed the spider. Sure enough, it was made of latex.

It's very realistic, thought Zac, impressed. *Whoever made it must have REALLY wanted to scare people away*. He dropped it into his backpack. It would come in handy the next time he wanted to play a joke on Leon.

Then Zac grabbed hold of the door handle. Time to start investigating. But the moment he began turning the handle, Zac heard a loud, spooky voice.

KEEEEEP OOOOOOUUT!

What IS that? thought Zac. He took his hand off the handle and the voice stopped.

Someone is up to something here, thought Zac, checking the door. Sure enough, he saw a wire running from the handle of the door, up along the doorframe and disappearing into the walls.

Zac shook his head and pushed open the door. The voice spoke again.

ABANDON ALL HOPE, YE WHO ENTER!

Yeah, whatever! Zac thought, stepping inside. He wasn't scared, but he was on full alert. Whoever was in here would definitely know that Zac was inside the mansion, after all the noise that door had made.

CHAPTER 4

Inside the mansion it was completely dark. But Zac could clearly make out that strange rustling sound he'd heard through the door before. Now he could hear squeaking, too.

As Zac's eyes adjusted to the darkness, he saw some strange shapes hanging from the roof beams.

Oh, gross, thought Zac. *I hate bats!*

He tip-toed quietly across the room, trying not to disturb them. But then he tripped over on the edge of a carpet.

CRASH!

Suddenly, the squeaking got incredibly loud. A moment later, Zac was mobbed by hundreds of cold, furious bats, flapping their wings in his face and screeching so loudly that he thought his eardrums would burst.

Zac tried to push his way through the angry bats. But then they swarmed together and linked up all their claws. Zac found himself facing one enormous super-bat!

There's no way I'm fighting that thing! thought Zac. There had to be a way to escape!

Then Zac remembered something Leon had said about a new feature on the SpyPad called the Sonic Scrambler.

'Bats have super-sensitive hearing,' Leon had explained. 'And they rely on sound to navigate. If you turn on the Sonic Scrambler, they'll go nuts!'

With one hand shielding his face from the super-bat's sharp claws, Zac quickly selected the Sonic Scrambler on his Spypad and pushed the button.

Nothing happened. Nothing that Zac could hear, anyway. It was a different

story for the bats. They instantly stopped squeaking and dropped out of the super-bat formation.

Then the bats started doing somersaults in the air at top speed, and crashing through a window to get outside. They moved so fast that they were nothing but a big, batty blur.

No real bat could move that fast, thought Zac, suspicious.

He reached out and grabbed one. It felt cold and hard – not like a living creature at all.

Sure enough, when Zac flipped the bat over, he saw 'AcroBat' stamped on the back. It was just a robot.

He let go of it and the AcroBat whizzed out the window with the others.

Right, thought Zac, checking the time on his watch. *What should I do now?*

6.04 P.M.

He decided to kill time by playing a few games on his SpyPad.

There's plenty of time to check out the mansion later, he figured, picking a dark corner and sitting down against the wall.

Zac yawned and opened his eyes. For a moment, he had no idea where he was. Then he remembered that he was crashing a BIG mission in a supposedly haunted mansion.

I must have fallen asleep, he thought, stretching. He stood up and checked the time on his watch.

4.17 A.M.

When Zac looked around, he saw a dusty wooden staircase leading upstairs.

I guess I'd better do some investigating, he thought. *I bet that staircase leads to the tower.*

Zac started climbing the stairs. He had to push his way through giant spider webs, which were thick and stickier than superglue.

He had only just reached the first floor when he heard something that made him freeze.

THUMP-THUMP-THUMP!

The noise was coming from the cupboard on the landing. Someone – or something – was in there, banging loudly.

THWHACK! THWHACK!

The banging was getting louder. Then another sound joined in.

WHOOOOOOO!

Zac gulped. *There's no such thing as ghosts*, he reminded himself. *I'll just open the cupboard and everything will be explained. It's not like a ghost is going to come floating out.*

Zac reached over and flung the cupboard door open.

WHOOOOOOO!

Instantly, a white shape rushed out of the cupboard. And it headed straight for Zac!

CHAPTER 5

Quickly, Zac grabbed hold of the white shape and yanked hard. It was just a sheet, and underneath was someone with a very familiar face.

'Caz?' Zac gasped.

Caz Rewop was the last person Zac ever wanted to run into on a mission. She was the sneakiest, meanest BIG agent Zac had ever met. *But hang on*, thought Zac, confused. *If this is Caz, why is she suddenly taller?*

'I'm not Caz,' said the girl, looking frightened. 'I'm her big sister. Who are you? What are you doing here?'

'Er, I'm here because I was sent a BIG mission,' said Zac.

'Oh, so you work for BIG, too!' said the girl, looking relieved. 'I'm so glad you're here. I've just joined BIG and this is my first solo mission. Everyone thinks that I'm going to be just as brilliant as Caz. But I'm not. I'm good at inventing gadgets, but I'm hopeless at dealing with haunted houses. It's way too scary!'

Then she smiled and stuck out her hand for Zac to shake. 'I'm Agent Gadget Girl,' she said, 'but just call me Leonie.'

She has no idea who I am, thought Zac. Perfect! Leonie could be a useful source of information for this mission.

'I'm, er, Agent Choir Boy,' said Zac, thinking fast. Zac's *real* code name was Agent Rock Star.

'Maybe we can work together?' suggested Leonie hopefully. 'I've got heaps of my own cool gadgets we can use. And the mansion's floor plans are on my SpyDevice – want to see?'

She stuck out her SpyDevice for Zac to have a look.

'Sure, let's work together. I was scared, too,' lied Zac as he checked out the floor plans. It seemed like the SpyDevice was the BIG version of a SpyPad.

'Cool bananas!' grinned Leonie.

Zac choked back a laugh. He couldn't help liking Leonie, even though she was a BIG agent and Caz's sister. The only other person who would say something as lame as 'cool bananas' was his own geeky brother.

'Let's go, then,' said Zac. 'I still haven't been up to the room at the top of the tower.'

But just then, they heard another sound.

HA-HA-HAAAH!

Leonie grabbed Zac's arm very tightly.

'I heard that spooky laughter before,' she whimpered. 'That's why I hid in the cupboard with a sheet over my head. I thought if a monster found me, they would think I was a ghost and leave me alone.'

'I think it's just someone trying to scare us,' said Zac.

'Well, it's working,' wailed Leonie. 'Let's leave!'

'No,' said Zac firmly. 'Let's go exploring.'

The sound was coming from behind a nearby door. Zac strode over.

'Don't open it!' pleaded Leonie.

I'll show her there's nothing to be afraid of, decided Zac, pushing open the door.

It sounded like a dinner party was going on in there. Zac could hear glasses clinking and cutlery scraping across plates. There was also a lot of laughing and talking. But it was too dark to see anything.

'Do you have a torch on you?' Zac whispered to Leonie.

'No, but I've got a Lightning Ball,' Leonie whispered back. She handed him something small and round, about the size a gobstopper. 'When it bounces, it makes a flash of light that lasts for about thirty seconds. But I think we should just leave now, while we still –'

'No, let's see what's going on,' replied Zac. Then he threw the Lightning Ball into the room. There was a bang, and instantly, the room lit up like someone had set off a flare.

In the middle of the room was a big table laid out for a dinner party with fine china and crystal glasses. And seated around the table were eight guests. Eight skeleton guests! They were cutting invisible food with their knives and lifting empty glasses up to their mouths as if they were drinking.

'Aaaaah!' shrieked Leonie.

CHAPTER

Instantly, all the skeletons started waving their bony arms towards Zac and Leonie, laughing nastily.

'Calm down, Leonie,' Zac hissed. 'It obviously can't be real. Have you got another light source?'

'Can't we just go?' whimpered Leonie.

'No,' said Zac firmly. 'We're staying.'

'Well, that was my last Lightning Ball,' sighed Leonie, 'but I've got a Fandle.'

'What's a Fandle?' asked Zac.

Leonie handed Zac what looked like a stick with a tiny, glowing light bulb on the top. On the side was a small rotor. A breeze blowing through the broken window was making it turn.

'The spinning fan powers the light,' explained Leonie.

'Nice!' said Zac, impressed.

He held the Fandle out and took a few steps towards the dinner party. The skeletons were still stretching out their arms and chortling. But Zac wasn't worried.

He examined the skeletons carefully. 'Just as I thought,' he told Leonie. 'They're puppets.'

Zac showed Leonie the wire attached to the skeletons' bones. 'See? These wires are connected to pulleys hidden up in the ceiling. There's a machine up there that's making them rise and fall so it looks like the skeletons are moving by themselves.'

'But what about the laughing and talking?' whispered Leonie, still scared.

Zac shone the Fandle over one of the bowls on the table. Hidden inside was a tiny wireless speaker.

'There you go,' he said. 'There's always a logical explanation.'

Oh, no, Zac thought to himself. He was beginning to sound like Leon!

'Um, Agent Choir Boy?' said Leonie, raising an eyebrow. 'What's the logical explanation for that?'

Zac turned and found himself staring right into the glowing red eyes of a large, purple floating blob. Actually, he was staring *through* it, as the blob was totally transparent. Zac gulped. This thing looked exactly like a ghost. But that wasn't possible, was it?

'Run!' shouted Leonie.

'It's probably just a hologram,' said Zac, more confidently than he felt. If it really was a hologram, it looked very realistic.

'It's not a hologram,' said Leonie. 'Holograms can't move through three-dimensional space like *that*!'

Zac glanced over his shoulder. Sure enough, the ghost had started gliding towards them!

Leonie took off down the dark corridor, and Zac followed. He wasn't scared, because he was pretty sure this thing was another trick. But he couldn't risk losing sight of Leonie. She had the gadgets, after all. And the map.

'Dead end,' called Leonie, stopping suddenly. 'We're doomed!'

Up ahead, the corridor was completely blocked by a floor-to-ceiling bookcase.

Zac stopped and looked around. The ghost hovered in front of them. Then Zac noticed something weird. The ghost was flickering, like it was being turned on and off.

Hang on, thought Zac, shining the Fandle around the corridor.

'Leonie, look!' he said, pointing.

There were rows of tiny lights in the floor. And there were heaps more in the ceiling and along the walls.

Leonie looked carefully at the lights. 'Wow,' she said, suddenly completely unafraid. 'This ghost is a volumetric display! You know, a hologram projected from six different directions.'

'Are you sure?' asked Zac. He could remember Leon once telling him something about this. 'I thought volumetric displays were only in the early stages of development.'

'Yeah, this is cutting-edge stuff,' said Leonie. 'And dangerous. So, what do we do now? I think we're stuck.'

Zac had to agree that things looked bad. On one side of them was the bookcase. On the other was the volumetric display ghost. There was no way Zac was pushing through that thing. The way it was buzzing and sparking told him that it was electrified.

He checked his watch.

5.55 A.M.

There were still four hours until the storm was due to strike and he had to be up in the tower.

What are we supposed to do until then? thought Zac, leaning heavily against the bookcase. *Just wait around until the ghost leaves us alone?*

The bookcase begin to shift, and before Zac could move, it had spun around like a revolving door. Then the ground gave way beneath his feet, and Zac fell heavily into the darkness.

CHAPTER 7

Zac blinked in the darkness and sat up
woozily. His head felt sore. He must have
bumped it on the way down. He guessed
he'd been passed out for an hour or two.

'Stupid revolving bookshelf!' he
muttered to himself. 'I should have seen
that coming.'

Zac looked around. The room was very

dark because there weren't any windows. The only light was coming from a vent near the ceiling.

I'm in the cellar, he realised.

Nearby was a stack of boxes. Instantly, Zac's spy senses started tingling. The boxes looked brand new – not like things that had been stored in a cellar for years and years. Zac inspected one of the box labels.

Fake Dust

Zac got up and opened the box. It was filled with a greyish, chalky powder. It looked exactly like real dust, but for some reason it smelt like flowers.

He read the label on the next box.

Instant Spider Webs

There were lots of bottles inside. When Zac took one and squeezed it, strings of clear glue shot out and attached themselves to the wall. They looked like the webs he'd fought through while climbing the stairs.

Hmmm, fake dust and fake spider webs, thought Zac. *Looks like someone's been trying really hard to make this place seem like an old haunted house.*

Nearby he could hear a low, humming noise. Zac tracked the sound to a large metal machine. Every now and then a little puff of steam came out of it and then disappeared through the ceiling vent.

It's some kind of generator, realised Zac. *But what is it for?*

Then he saw a little label on the side of the machine. He crouched down to read it. It said: *StormGenerator BIG-prototype DC76/14.* Zac's skin crawled. BIG were making the storms! So why would they send their *own* agent to investigate?

Just then, a trapdoor in the ceiling burst open and a figure dropped through.

'Agent Choir Boy?' whispered a familiar voice. 'Are you in here?'

'Over here, Leonie,' Zac called out.

Leonie rushed over. 'I've been searching for you everywhere!' she exclaimed. 'One minute you were standing right beside me and then suddenly you'd disappeared. It's taken me ages to find you.'

Then there was a rumble of thunder and a crash of lightning.

'There's a big storm coming,' Leonie said nervously. 'We should probably stay down here till it passes.'

Zac glanced at his watch. He had to be in the room at the top of the tower when the storm hit!

8.00 A.M.

'Leonie, we have to get up to the tower room,' said Zac urgently. 'Remember the mission? We're supposed to be up there when the storm breaks. And it sounds like the storm's coming now!'

'I'm not going anywhere,' Leonie whispered, terrified.

Zac sighed. *If only Leonie were a bit braver*, he thought. Then he remembered something. At Agent Hammer's birthday party last week, Zac had got a packet of fake No-Fear Gum in the lollybag.

Of course there was no such thing as *real* No-Fear Gum, but the idea was that whoever chewed the gum instantly looked tougher. And if they looked tougher, they felt tougher.

It's just what Leonie needs, thought Zac.

He looked through his backpack to find the lollybag.

'Hey, Leonie,' said Zac, taking out the gum and offering her a piece. 'Do you want some No-Fear Gum? It's special, er,

BIG-issue. It's supposed to stop you feeling scared.'

Leonie looked doubtful, but took a piece anyway.

'Hey, I think it's working,' she said as she started chewing. 'Maybe we should go up to the tower after all.' She jumped to her feet. 'Come on, I'll use my DOLL to find out if there's a secret passage in here.'

'Your doll?' said Zac. 'Aren't you a bit old for dolls?'

'DOLL is short for Door Or Lock Locator,' said Leonie, opening her bag and taking out what looked like a creepy doll. 'If it's pointed at a secret passage or concealed entrance, the eyes light up. Watch.'

Leonie swung the DOLL around the room. Sure enough, after a few moments, the eyes started flashing.

Zac shuddered. 'That's the scariest thing I've seen all day,' he said under his breath.

Leonie raced over to one of the walls and gave it a whack with the DOLL. Instantly, a panel slid back, revealing a narrow entrance with steps leading up.

Leonie pulled out her SpyDevice and checked the map. 'These steps lead right up to the tower room,' she said, putting her SpyDevice away. 'Are you ready, Agent Choir Boy?'

'Let's do it,' said Zac firmly.

CHAPTER 8

Leonie bounced up the stairs, still chewing on the fake No-Fear Gum. 'Hurry up!' she barked over her shoulder.

Zac rolled his eyes. The new, super-brave Leonie was also super bossy!

Then Zac spotted something that froze him to the spot. Up ahead was a figure, lurking in the shadows.

'Wait, Leonie,' he warned. 'It could be an ambush.'

But Leonie laughed and kept going. 'It's just an old suit of armour!' she said, shining the Fandle on the figure.

But Zac's spy senses were still on full alert. 'Don't touch it,' he told her.

'I can't believe that this time you're scared and I'm not!' giggled Leonie, knocking on the suit with her knuckles.

Then the knight raised one arm and pushed Leonie over.

SWAT!

'Aaah!' squealed Leonie, tumbling backwards.

Zac leapt forwards and caught her.

In one hand, the knight held a gleaming sword. In the other was a spiky ball and chain, which it was whizzing around over its head. The knight took a threatening step towards them.

'Got anything that might help us out here, Leonie?' muttered Zac.

'Just this,' said Leonie, pulling out her hairclip. 'It's a super-strong magnet.'

'Great!' said Zac, impressed.

'On the count of three,' said Leonie. 'One, two ... three!'

Zac ran up and grabbed the knight's legs, while Leonie slipped the magnet onto one of its knees. The magnet instantly stuck the knight's legs together.

'Run!' yelled Leonie, heading up the stairs.

Zac wasn't far behind. But a moment later…

CLUNK!

Leonie and Zac leapt up the stairs two at a time. But the knight was dragging itself up the stairs behind them.

CLANK! CLUNK! CLANK!

There was a door at the top of the stairs. That must be the door to the tower room, thought Zac. He rattled the handle, but it was locked.

'What do we do now?' asked Leonie.

Thinking quickly, Zac fished around in his pocket and pulled out his keys.

Door key, bike key, locker key, thought Zac, flipping through them.

Finally, he found what he was looking for – a skeleton key. It was meant to open almost any door in the world. Leon had given it to him ages ago, but Zac had never tried it out before.

'Hurry!' warned Leonie. 'The knight's coming closer!'

Zac could still hear the clanking sound of the knight dragging itself up the stairs. He stuck the skeleton key into the lock. It turned, but then got stuck and refused to budge.

The clanking sound grew louder and louder. Then suddenly Leonie leapt down a few steps towards the knight and karate-kicked it away.

'Heee-YA!' she yelled.

The knight fell back down the stairs with a huge crash.

'I didn't know you knew karate!' said Zac, raising an eyebrow.

'I don't,' grinned Leonie.

Zac shook his head and laughed. Maybe that No-Fear Gum was real, after all!

He forced the skeleton key to twist in the lock, and finally the door opened. Zac and Leonie flung themselves into the room and banged the door shut behind them.

The room was dark and smelt strongly of flowers. In fact, it smelt like lavender.

Just like that fake dust, realised Zac. *And that little old lady who told me not to come in here!*

Leonie nudged him. 'Um, Agent Choir Boy?' she muttered. 'We're not alone.'

She pointed to a big chair in the middle of the room. It was rocking backwards and forwards.

Slowly, the chair swung around.

CHAPTER

'Welcome, agents,' said the person in the chair. 'Congratulations on passing the test.'

It was the sweet old lady he'd met the day before. But her weird purple hair was gone, and she was wearing a BIG uniform!

Zac shot a look at Leonie. Did she know who this BIG person was?

Leonie was standing to attention. 'Agent

Gadget Girl at your service, Commander Big Wig!' she said excitedly. 'What's the test?'

'This whole mansion is one big test,' replied Commander Big Wig smoothly. 'It was created to trial BIG's top-secret new scaring technology.'

Zac's mind was ticking over. *Of course my SpyPad didn't intercept that BIG mission — it didn't even have a signal!* He realised that BIG must have scrambled his reception and then planted the message.

'You wanted us to come here as guinea pigs,' said Zac, shaking his head.

'Exactly, Agent Rock Star,' smiled Big Wig. 'But you and Gadget Girl are the first agents to actually make it to the top.'

'Hang on,' frowned Leonie. 'This is Agent Choir Boy, not Agent Rock Star.'

'Wrong,' said Big Wig. 'Obviously, the ultimate test of our scaring technology would be if it worked on GIB agents. That's why we sent the mission to Agent Rock Star, the most fearless spy in the business.'

Leonie stared at Zac. 'You're a GIB agent?'

'Well, yes,' Zac admitted.

'You lied to me!' yelled Leonie.

'Enough bickering,' growled the Commander. 'I haven't finished telling you about this place!'

Zac's mind was going a million miles

an hour. Why was Big Wig so keen to tell them about the mansion if it was secret technology? And how was he going to get out of there?

'The whole place is powered by storm energy,' explained the Commander proudly. 'That storm generator in the cellar creates the storm clouds over the mansion, which then makes thunder and lightning. The lightning zaps a power-grid on the roof and sends electricity surging through the entire building.'

Then Zac realised something. 'Is that why all the city's appliances have been on the blink recently?' he asked. 'Because you're generating so much electricity here?'

'Correct,' grinned Big Wig nastily. 'And we've been able to use it to manipulate your private mobile networks, Rock Star. Tell me, does your SpyPad have a signal yet?'

Zac said nothing. He knew it didn't.

Commander Big Wig turned to Leonie. 'Agent Gadget Girl, as you've passed the test, you will now be made a BIG field agent.'

Leonie looked proud. *She won't be a fearless field agent once she stops chewing that fake No-Fear Gum*, thought Zac, annoyed.

'What about you, Rock Star?' smirked Big Wig. 'I can make you an official BIG field agent too, if you want.'

'No way!' snapped Zac. 'Firstly, I'm not a girl like your other agents. And secondly, I'm not evil.'

'Your stupidity is disappointing,' snarled Big Wig, 'but predictable. Which is why I installed this.'

She pointed at the ceiling. There was a clear sheet of glass, and through that, Zac could see what looked like a telescope on a mechanical arm. It was mounted on the roof.

'What is it?' asked Leonie.

'It's called the Statue-Maker,' replied Big Wig. 'Did you notice our sculpture garden out the front?'

'You mean the trees and flowers that

were like stone?' asked Zac.

'Yes,' nodded Big Wig. 'We've discovered that if you capture lightning correctly, you can concentrate the electrons to fuse molecules together. It's sort of like drying glue really quickly. I've been testing it on all our plants, but you will have the honour of being the first person we test it on.'

'What a cool gadget!' Leonie marvelled.

Zac glared at her. She was becoming more evil like Caz every second!

'Come on, Gadget Girl,' said Big Wig. 'We're leaving. Rock Star will stay locked in this tower. I can control the Statue-Maker from outside with my remote.

When the storm hits, Zac will be turned into a statue!'

Rain began to patter on the windows. Lightning rumbled in the sky.

'There's that storm now,' smirked Big Wig, flicking a switch. The Statue-Maker began to buzz. 'Goodbye, Rock Star.'

Big Wig and Leonie marched towards the door.

'Bye, Choir Boy,' said Leonie. 'I'll say hi to Caz for you.'

Then she pulled the door shut behind them, and Zac heard a key turning in the lock.

CHAPTER 10

Once the door was shut, Zac swung into action. He'd left the skeleton key in the lock, so he knew he couldn't get out through the door. And the lightning strikes were getting closer. There wasn't a second to waste!

Zac raced to the window and tried opening it. Luckily, it was unlocked.

Zac looked outside. The ground was a long way down – definitely too far to jump. But Zac had an idea. He pulled out the lollybag from Agent Hammer's party and rifled through it.

It didn't take him long to find what he was looking for. A mini bungy cord! It was ultra lightweight, but also ultra strong.

Zac quickly hooked one end of the bungy cord onto the window frame. Outside, the clouds were growing darker.

OK, here goes, he thought, knotting the other end of the bungy cord to his belt buckle. He climbed out the window frame, took a big breath, and then jumped.

Zac fell through the air. Just before he

hit the ground, the bungy tightened and tossed him back up.

SPROING!

Zac bounced up and down a few times before finally coming to a stop.

Dangling just a metre from the ground, Zac untied the bungy cord and dropped down. Then he dashed towards the front gate. He had to get out of there!

RUMMMMBLE!

The sky turned silver as a massive bolt of lightning hit the house. There was a creaking, groaning noise. Zac looked over his shoulder as he ran.

Whoah! he thought, almost tripping over his own feet.

The lightning had split the house apart. The whole mansion was collapsing! Sparks flew everywhere, like fireworks.

Then Zac noticed two dusty figures running from the rubble. It was Commander Big Wig and Leonie. He was relieved they were OK, even though they worked for BIG. Zac didn't like to see people get hurt.

'What happened?' he heard Leonie whimper. Suddenly she didn't seem quite so brave.

'The controls on the Statue-Maker must have been up too high!' growled the Commander. 'It short-circuited the entire house and blew it up. That's two years of

research ruined! But at least we've got rid of that pesky Zac Power.'

'Help!' Leonie squealed suddenly.

Zac laughed as he watched from behind the front gate. The knight had survived the collapse, too. It was chasing Leonie around, waving its sword in the air.

'Show some guts, Agent Gadget Girl,' snapped Big Wig.

'I can't,' cried Leonie. 'I've swallowed my No-Fear Gum!'

Zac turned away from the house and caught sight of the Dragonfly Commuter-Scooter parked across the street.

Cool, he thought. *Looks like I've got my ride home!*

There was one final burst of sparks from the rubble of the haunted house, and then everything went quiet. The storm clouds were fading away.

Zac's SpyPad beeped to show it had finally picked up a signal. As Zac climbed onto the scooter, he called Leon to tell him he was on his way home.

'Glad to hear you're safe, Zac,' said Leon. 'Nice work, too.'

Zac nodded. It was only 9.30 a.m., so he still had heaps of time to relax before he went and saw the movie Ghost Fighter with his friends.

Awesome, thought Zac. He suddenly felt hungry. *And I want breakfast, too.*

'Oh, one more thing,' added Leon through the SpyPad. 'I haven't finished installing all those energy-saving light bulbs. You've got to help me before you go see your movie!'

Zac groaned. He really didn't feel like dealing with light bulbs right now. But a promise was a promise. He said goodbye to Leon and hung up.

Oh well, at least I can scare Leon with that fake huntsman spider I found, Zac grinned to himself as he revved the Dragonfly scooter. *Should make changing light bulbs a bit more interesting!*

KABOOM!
ZAC POWER
4 MISSIONS IN 1!
ZAC'S BIGGEST HITS!
H.I. LARRY
VOLUME ONE

ZAC'S BIGGEST HITS!

VOLUME ONE

COMPUTER HACKERS, PIRANHAS,
THE NORTH POLE AND HOLLYWOOD –
ZAC'S **BIGGEST** ADVENTURES ARE
ACTION-PACKED! CAN HE SURVIVE
BIG'S DIRTY TRICKS AND SAVE
THE WORLD AGAIN?

A THRILLING SUPER-SET OF FOUR SPY ADVENTURES:

MIND GAMES · BLOCKBUSTER
POISON ISLAND · FROZEN FEAR

ZAC'S EVEN BIGGER HITS!

VOLUME TWO

EVIL ROCKSTARS, ROBOTIC CROCODILES, ERUPTING VOLCANOS AND PARACHUTE PANTS – ZAC'S **EVEN BIGGER** ADVENTURES ARE ACTION-PACKED! BUT ARE HIS SPY SKILLS GOOD ENOUGH TO SAVE THE WORLD ... AGAIN AND AGAIN?

AN EXCITING SUPER-SET OF FOUR SPY ADVENTURES:

VOLCANIC PANIC · SKY HIGH SHOCK MUSIC · SWAMP RACE

AXEL & BEAST

One elite gamer. One shape-shifting robot. Unlimited adventure!

When a shape-shifting robot needs help to save the world, it's time for this young gamer to level up!

One day, Axel is playing video games when something **HUGE** breaks into his garage. It's a robot. His name is **BEAST**. And he's on the run from the nasty Grabbem Industries, who want **BEAST** back!

Axel and **BEAST** can't wait to go on their first real mission together. And when it finally comes through, it's a killer!

The evil Grabbem Industries are illegally drilling for oil in the Antarctic – but how are they getting away with it?

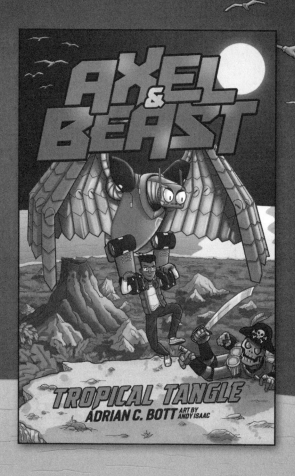

Grabbem Industries are having a blast on a tropical island – a **NUCLEAR** blast!

Axel and **BEAST** have to stop them no matter what. But what if it means splitting up?

The rumours of a super-powerful reactor buried under Ghost Island are **TRUE** – and Grabbem Industries want it for themselves!

Axel and **BEAST** are racing to keep it out of Grabbem's hands. But could the rumours of a guardian monster be true too?

When Agent Omega goes missing inside Grabbem's headquarters, Axel and **BEAST** have to rescue him. But can they make it in – and **OUT** – without getting caught?

AXEL & BEAST
CASTLE OF CYBORGS
ADRIAN C. BOTT ART BY ANDY ISAAC

Axel and **BEAST** must journey to
the Neuron Institute, where the evil
Professor Payne is fusing man with machines.
Can they fight off cyberwolves, robotic angels
and the dreaded **MONSTER** in the dungeon
to complete their biggest mission yet:

saving Axel's dad?